Chicory is Trickery

A Spicetown Mystery

Sheri Richey

Sheri Richey

For further information, contact the publisher: Amazon Publishing.

The author assumes no responsibility for errors or omissions that are inadvertent or inaccurate. This is a work of fiction and is not intended to reflect actual events or persons.

ISBN: 9781648717406

Cover art by Mariah Sinclair

Spicetown Mysteries

Welcome to Spicetown
A Bell in the Garden
Spilling the Spice
Blue Collar Bluff
A Tough Nut to Crack
Chicory is Trickery

Romance by Sheri Richey:

The Eden Hall Series:
Finding Eden
Saving Eden
Healing Eden
Protecting Eden
Completing Eden
∞
Willow Wood

Sheri Richey

CHAPTER 1

Cora Mae pulled the collar of her coat closer together when the chilly breeze made her shiver. The bright sunshine had tricked her outside, but the wind was giving her cause to regret that decision.

"Morning, Mayor." Harvey Salzman waved a gloved hand as he stepped off the curb to cross Fennel Street where it intercepted with Clove Street. His other arm hugged a brown box and his cheeks were rosy from the wind.

"Good morning, Saucy. What are you up to today?"

"Ah, just running a little errand for Miss Fields at the library. She asked me to drop this off with Peggy at the Carom Seed Craft Corner."

"Well, it's chillier than I expected, but it's a beautiful day. I'm so glad the rain from last night didn't linger."

"Isn't March supposed to come in like a lion and out like a lamb?" Saucy poked his index finger into his cheek. "Or do I have that backwards?"

"No, you're right, Saucy." Cora Mae chuckled as she waited for the traffic light to turn green so she could cross Clove Street. "I'm afraid the lamb may have gotten lost in the last snowfall we had." Saucy's laughter caused his box to teeter back and forth under his arm, and Cora reached out to steady it. "Is your box heavy?"

"Oh, no. It's just bulky. Are you going down Fennel Street?"

"No, I'm dropping off my taxes with Jacob Hart. Have you done your taxes yet, Saucy?"

"Yes, ma'am." Saucy switched his box to his other arm. "Mine were in the mail in early February."

"As usual, you are on top of everything. I've been putting it off and time is running out."

"I'm sure Jacob will get it done for you." Saucy held his arm out and pointed across Clove Street. "It doesn't look like they're open yet."

Cora Mae glanced down the side street and saw the closed sign hanging inside the door to Hart & Grace Tax Services. "You're right, Saucy. I called early this morning and left a voice mail that I was coming by today, but I thought they opened at ten o'clock."

"Maybe he's sick," Saucy said with a shrug of his shoulders. "There's always something going around this time of year."

"Both of them!" Cora huffed. "Well, I guess I'll try them again tomorrow, but next time I'll call first."

Saucy nodded as Cora waved before scurrying off towards Paprika Parkway.

Upon returning to City Hall, Cora tossed her coat on the hook behind her door and rubbed her hands together. "That was a chilly walk and I didn't accomplish a thing."

"Mr. Hart wasn't there?" Amanda Morgan called out as she walked towards Cora's office door.

"Nobody was there. Hart & Grace was closed. I can't imagine why neither of them came into the office this morning. This should be their busiest time of year."

"Is it just Mr. Grace and Mr. Hart? No one else works there?"

"No, just the two men. I've seen Tim's wife, Tonya, in there a few times helping out, but I don't think it's a regular thing."

"It's too early for lunch," Amanda said.

"Do you do your own taxes?" Cora Mae propped her elbow on her desk and cupped her chin in the palm of her hand.

"I do," Amanda said as she slid into the chair across from Cora's desk. "Mine are really simple. I'm a little worried about Bryan's this year, though. I told him I would help him, but he may have to take his stuff to Hart & Grace if we can't figure it out."

"I'm ashamed to admit I've never even tried." Cora logged into her computer and spun around in her chair. "Bing always took care of that, and after he died, I took everything to Jacob Hart. If he doesn't show up, I may have to try my hand at it."

"I told Bryan we would look at that this weekend. He keeps putting it off. He started Stotlar Nursery at the beginning of last year and I told him to save everything. I don't know what records he needs."

"I don't know anything about business taxes." Cora shoved her purse into her bottom drawer. "I would think he could write off a lot of his costs from opening the plant nursery, but he was self-employed even before that when he did the Christmas trees. Who did his taxes last year?"

"That's a good question." Amanda looked around nervously. "I'll have to find out."

"Both of your parents are self-employed. Who does their taxes?"

"That's another good question." Amanda smiled. "I hadn't even thought about it and I don't think I've ever heard them mention it."

"Well, it worries me because I've called Jacob several times and I keep getting voice mail. I know it's my fault for waiting this late, but I never imagined he wouldn't be there. Let me know what you find out because I may be looking for someone else."

"I will." Amanda flipped open the file folder in her hand. "But Mayor, we have an Easter egg dilemma."

"Oh, no. We can't get them?"

"Not the same ones we used last year. I called the company and they don't sell those anymore. I found another distributor, but it's going to cost a little more."

"We've got to think of a way to recycle these eggs back to City Hall after the egg hunts. We can't keep buying two thousand eggs every year. The City Council is cutting every corner they find, and I'll surely lose my Easter Eggs-Travaganza once they notice the cost increase."

"I'll keep looking for options." Amanda jumped from the chair when she heard the phone ring and Cora nodded.

Reaching for her mouse, Cora clicked open a browser window and searched for plastic Easter eggs. Perhaps there were options out there that Amanda might have missed.

"Mayor," Amanda called out from her adjoining office. "The Chief's on the phone."

"Okay," Cora hollered as she grabbed at the phone on her desk. "Hey, Connie. I thought you were going to be in Paxton all day today."

"Nah, I'm driving back now. Georgia told me you called this morning."

"I did." Cora said, turning back to her desk. "I just wanted to tell you that I'm making chili tonight and you're welcome to stop by if you want. I was planning to text you later this afternoon."

"That sounds good. I'll be there!"

"It should be ready by six o'clock. Did you have court today?"

"No, I had a doctor's appointment." Conrad huffed. "I think the guy's a quack."

Cora Mae giggled. "Now, what makes you think that?"

"He can't find anything wrong with me, and then he tells me to quit drinking coffee. Now, exactly what good would that do me? If I quit drinking coffee, there'll be a whole lot more wrong with me."

"Perhaps, but everyone else will suffer along with you."

"He wants me to go without coffee for two weeks and then come back and see him. I guess if I'm not better, he'll have me give up meat next. We'll just keep sacrificing all the things that have meaning in my life until he finds the right thing."

"You're already grumpy and you haven't even tried to make it a day without coffee yet." Cora laughed. "Is it the caffeine he wants you to avoid? If so, there's always decaf."

"Ack!" Conrad gasped. "That's brown water. I can't take that. I'd rather do without."

"Oh, my. It's going to be a long two weeks."

§

As he drove, Conrad listened to his dispatcher, Georgia Marks, calling out to Officer Hudson to drive out to the new construction site to address a dispute. Conrad groaned when he heard Georgia give Lavender Lane as the address.

Miriam Landry, the unpopular President of the Spicetown Chamber of Commerce, had subdivided a plot of farmland on the north side of town and several new homes were under construction. Adjacent to her subdivision was Cumin Court, which was another new subdivision owned by a real estate company in Columbus, Ohio. Miriam was in a constant dispute with various contractors in her subdivision and the neighboring lots, just as she was in regular dispute with the citizens of Spicetown. She was an exhausting woman.

"Georgia," Conrad barked into his console after calling the office through his car Bluetooth.

"Yeah, Chief."

"I'm almost back to town. I'll stop by and check on Miriam."

"Thanks, Chief."

Conrad heard Georgia cancel her call to Officer Hudson over the police radio and he growled. Miriam needed to keep her temper in check because she was wasting city resources with all this nonsense. As he turned into Lavender Lane, he scanned the parked cars for Doug Keegan's truck. Doug had been hired by Miriam to manage the subdivision development, but Miriam wasn't letting him do his job. Coasting between the trucks lining the sides of the lane, he saw Miriam's Cadillac parked at the end of the street and pulled over next to it. Bryan Stotlar was unloading a tree from the back of his truck at one of the houses, and Conrad waved to him as he pulled up.

"Hey, Bryan," Conrad called out as he pushed his car door shut. "How are you today?"

"Great, Chief," Bryan said as he wiped his hand on his sweatshirt before extending it to shake. "Just setting up a tree here for Mr. Grace. How are things with you?"

"Good. Good." Conrad nodded his head and glanced down the street. "Any trouble out here today?"

"Nah, not that I know of, but I just got here."

"Have you seen Miriam Landry or Doug Keegan?"

"Doug is in the house," Bryan said, pointing at Tim Grace's home. "I haven't seen Mrs. Landry."

"Okay, thanks." Conrad walked across the dirt lawn of Tim Grace's new construction. The home was under roof, but with no interior walls or windows yet, Conrad could see several people inside working.

"Chief!" Doug Keegan stood in the doorway and waved. "Did you bring Briscoe?" Conrad's dog and best detective, Briscoe, was very fond of Doug's rescue pup, Doozie. Before the construction area had become congested, Conrad had allowed Briscoe some running time with Doozie in the empty lots.

"Not today. He's back at the station. I just stopped by because we got a call about a dispute. Do you know what's going on?"

Doug's chest heaved as he released a sigh. "No, but it's probably two houses down. That's where Miriam is right now. I'll walk down there with you."

As Doug stepped down from the house, Conrad turned to follow him. "Why is she out here?" Conrad shook his head. "She's not building herself, so I don't understand why she's getting involved."

"This house down here belongs to a friend of hers and she's trying to make sure things are done correctly. I think the contractor is about to quit on her, though. I've tried to warn her that this isn't the way to deal with general contractors, but—"

"She can't help herself," Conrad said. "I didn't think she had any friends. Who's the owner?"

"Her husband's friend, maybe." Doug chuckled. "She drops in almost every day."

"Hello? Miriam?" Conrad stepped into the house gingerly. Walking heavily across the plywood flooring, he heard voices raised in the back of the house.

"You can't quit!"

Conrad followed Miriam Landry's screech. "Miriam?" Conrad found them in the back of the house.

"I don't have a contract with you, lady."

Conrad approached a short, stocky man with his hands on his hips. "Excuse me." Conrad extended his hand to the gentleman. "I'm Chief Harris. I got a call about—"

"You didn't get a call from me," the man barked. "Sorry. Herb Upchurch, general contractor."

Conrad shook his hand and continued to ignore Miriam, who was in her usual state of rage. "Nice to meet you. I'm not sure who the call was from, but they said there was a disturbance."

"You're looking at it." Herb extended his arm and pointed his index finger at Miriam Landry.

"Miriam, can I have a word with you?" Conrad turned to lock eyes with Miriam and nodded toward the front entrance.

Miriam huffed and stomped to the front door opening of the house where her husband, Gerald, was waiting for her.

"Let's step outside." Conrad walked down the temporary steps and halfway to the street before turning around to wait on Miriam.

"Miriam, did you call the station?"

"No, Conrad. I didn't. This isn't anything that concerns you. I'm trying to keep this stupid man from making a costly mistake and he won't listen to me."

"Whose house is this?" Conrad glanced over to Gerald as he walked up behind Miriam.

"I called you, Conrad." Gerald stepped up beside Miriam and pretended not to see Miriam's snarling glare. "I'm sorry. I was afraid this guy, Upchurch, was going to get out of hand. He's not been very easy to deal with and things were getting heated."

"It's okay, Gerald. I understand. It's just that we get called out here almost every day and there has to be another solution to these ongoing problems. Whose house is this? I don't understand your involvement here."

"It's Jacob Hart's house and he asked us to keep an eye on things for him. He's too busy right now to oversee this and we told him we'd help out." Miriam pushed her shoulders back. "That little man in there knows that and he refuses to cooperate."

"What is he doing wrong? Is it something you can relay to Jacob, so he can contact him later about it?"

"I've left Jacob a voice mail. The man is putting up the walls today and he needs to be stopped right now. He was supposed to mirror the blueprints." Miriam held up her hands and crossed them. "Switch the rooms the opposite way and he's not doing that."

"Well, I don't think you are going to get anywhere by yelling at him. He's obviously not going to make changes based on what you're telling him. Maybe you both should go back to town and find Jacob. I'm sure once he calls Mr. Upchurch, they can work this out, assuming what you say is in the contract."

"He's right, Miriam." Gerald reached out and touched Miriam's elbow.

"I don't know where Jacob is, and I have every right to be here." Miriam jerked her elbow from Gerald's hold. "I thought the man would listen to reason. I will certainly make sure he doesn't get any future contracts in *my* subdivision."

"Now, Miriam. Let's just go see if we can get a hold of Jacob. He usually eats at the Caraway Café for lunch. Let's go get some lunch ourselves and see if we can catch him there." Gerald tried again to coax Miriam toward the street. "Thanks, Conrad. Sorry to drag you out here."

"Good to see you, Gerald." Conrad tipped his head down as they walked toward the street.

"I have to admit," Doug Keegan said as he strolled up. "Upchurch is a bit surly, so he's probably not the best guy to lock horns with Miriam."

"If you don't stand up to her, she'll walk all over you." Conrad shrugged his shoulders and shook his head. Gerald Landry must be a saint."

"I know." Doug Keegan waved as Conrad walked toward his car. "See you later, Chief."

CHAPTER 2

"Amanda, I'm going to drive over to the Caraway Café and get some lunch. Would you like me to bring you something?"

"No, thank you, Mayor. I have something here."

"Okay, dear. I may stop in at Hart & Grace if they're open, but I shouldn't be too late." Cora stuffed her tax folder into her large satchel handbag and reached for her coat.

"I do need to run this ad over to the newspaper before two o'clock," Amanda said as she glanced at the clock on the wall. "Oh, and you have a hair appointment this afternoon."

"Today? I thought it was Friday at four." Cora started scrolling through her calendar on her phone.

"It was, but mom called Monday and asked if she could move you to two o'clock today."

"You're right. You told me that and I didn't change it in my phone. That's actually a better time for me, anyway. Things may be hectic on

Friday afternoon if those eggs don't show up. Did you get a delivery confirmation?"

"I did, and they know we need them right away. The candy order should arrive tomorrow, but I was wondering..."

"Wondering what?" Cora paused before putting her arm in her coat.

"Well, you said we needed to figure out a way to get the kids to return the eggs." Amanda's eyes squinted as she wrinkled her nose. "What if we don't put anything inside of them this year?"

Cora Mae raised her eyebrows and smiled. "I don't think we'd have any trouble getting the eggs back then. I think the kids will throw them at us!"

Amanda blushed as Cora's laughter bellowed out when Jimmy Kole stuck his head in the doorway.

"Ladies! You are having entirely too much fun in a government building." Jimmy smiled as he zipped up his jacket.

"You know City Hall is the exception! How are you today?" Cora dropped her phone in her purse and slipped on her coat.

"Good! I'm just headed out for lunch and wanted to check on Operation Easter. I need to do a schedule for the guys. Do you know when the eggs will be ready?"

"We were just discussing eggs. They aren't all here yet, and the candy should come tomorrow. The hunt starts at ten o'clock. How long does it take to hide two thousand eggs?" Cora Mae looked at the ceiling and hummed.

"I think they can do it in two hours. I'm planning to schedule eight workers and two trucks. One to bring the eggs and the other to bring the tables for the vendors. We'll get started at seven."

Jimmy Kole was in charge of Spicetown Streets & Alleys, but his staff handled all the general maintenance for the city events. Cora had witnessed numerous occasions when some of his staff members would volunteer, even when there was no overtime available. He had a good crew.

"Good idea," Amanda said. "Then we'll have some extra time before any of the kids show up. The vendors will be there early to set up, but they shouldn't be in your way."

"Who is the Easter bunny this year?" Cora wrapped her scarf around her neck.

Jimmy Kole looked quizzically at Amanda. "I thought Marvin Goddard was always the Easter bunny."

"Oh, Marvin and his wife moved to Florida last year. Cece Fields said she would have to find a new bunny and I haven't heard from her. Have you, Amanda?"

"I've talked to her, but she didn't mention who was playing the part this year. She has a photographer coming to the library Saturday afternoon to offer the kids pictures with the Easter bunny, so she must have found a volunteer."

"I wonder who it could be." Cora Mae frowned and tossed her purse over her shoulder. "Well, I'm off to lunch, too. We'll let you know, Jimmy, as soon as everything comes in."

"Okay, Mayor. You guys have a good day." Jimmy Kole waved as he headed down the back hallway to the employee parking lot.

§

Cora Mae reached to pull the heavy glass door open at the Caraway Café, but before she could move aside, Miriam Landry pushed her way through the door. Startled, Cora jumped to the side as Gerald Landry followed behind Miriam. "Sorry. Hello, Mayor. How are you?"

"Oh, I'm just fine. It's good to see you, Gerald."

Gerald Landry waved his hand over his shoulder as he hurried to keep up with his wife. As usual, Miriam did not give Cora even the slightest glance.

Finding a table near the window to keep an eye on the street traffic, Cora pulled out her phone to change her hair appointment in her calendar. She had grown very dependent on that reminder application.

"Hi, Mayor. Can I take your order?" Jason Marks smiled as he held his order pad against his chest.

"Oh, Jason! I haven't seen you in a while. How are you?"

"I'm doing great, Mayor. I've been spending more time in the back with Frank. I'm learning a lot from him." Frank Parish ran the kitchen at the Caraway Café.

"Are you interested in becoming a chef?" Jason shrugged shyly. "I don't think so. It's hard work, but I do like to cook."

"Well, you are learning from one of the best! Frank Parish makes the best chicken salad in town."

Jason laughed. "Yeah, it's my mom's favorite, too." Jason's mother, Georgia Marks, was one of Spicetown's police dispatchers.

"I'm quite a fan, but today I think I want the club sandwich instead."

Jason nodded as he made a note on his pad. "That's our special today!"

Cora had seen that on the sign near the door and thought she might try something different. It was never good to get in a rut.

"Coming right up," Jason said as he tapped his pen before he put it in his apron pocket.

"I don't see Dot anywhere," Cora said. "Is Dorothy not in today?" Dorothy Parish, Frank's wife, managed the customer service side of the café.

"Oh, yeah. She just ran lunches out to the workers in the new subdivision."

"She's doing deliveries now?"

"Not all the time, but we added a lunch delivery just to that area, because there are so many workers out there. They call their orders in by eleven o'clock and then she just makes one trip out there. I think she's having fun meeting all the new people, but it's just temporary. We're not doing deliveries otherwise. We need her here during the day."

"Well, I can't imagine the café running smoothly without her. I'm sorry I missed her." Cora turned her cup over and placed her napkin over her lap.

"I'll tell her you were here. Let me get your tea." Jason scurried off to put in Cora's order.

Looking out the front windows of the Caraway Café, Cora saw a customer pull open the door to Spicetown Blooms & Gifts across the street. She hadn't been in the flower shop in months and wasn't sure who was running the store since Hazel Redding left Spicetown. The town did need a flower shop though, and she was happy to see that the business continued to thrive.

Once Jason brought her tea to the table, she saw Police Chief Conrad Harris come through the front door. "Hey Connie! Looking for lunch? I just ordered."

"Well, I called my lunch in. I was just going to pick it up and take it back to the office, but I'm in no hurry." Conrad waved to Jason and walked over to Cora's table. "I was a little afraid to come in here. I knew Miriam Landry was headed this way. I've already been out to her subdivision this morning."

"Oh, dear. Another disturbance?"

"Yes. Now she's fighting with the contractor Jacob Hart hired. She said she was headed this way looking for Jacob. Is he in here?"

"No. I didn't see him, but you're right. He is in here a lot at lunchtime. I was going to stop by his office after lunch. I'm still trying to get my paperwork to him."

"He does your taxes?"

"Yes, every year. I'm usually not this late, but I have been putting it off. I'm a little concerned because I haven't been able to catch him. I went by this morning and Hart & Grace wasn't open."

"Well, Miriam got into a fight with Jacob's contractor this morning. She said Jacob asked Gerald to keep an eye on things for him. I guess they're buddies. Miriam and Gerald can't find him either."

"My goodness! I can't imagine where he could be. He's usually in the office early in the morning. I'm going to go by there after I have lunch and see if I can catch him. He hasn't returned my calls either. He may be drowning in work. Tax time is just around the corner. Who does your taxes?"

"I do my own taxes. I always have."

"Is it easy? I've never tried it."

"It's not much fun, but it's not hard. It's all on computer now."

"Bing always did our taxes, and after he died, I didn't know what to do. Jacob offered to help, and I took everything to him."

"I wouldn't think you'd have any trouble doing your own now."

"I may have to try it, if I can't find him. I don't want to wait until the last minute. I will be a nervous wreck."

"It was always a privacy thing with me," Conrad said. "I didn't want to give my personal information to anybody. I'm funny about that, you know."

"In today's world, it's probably not a good idea, unless it's someone that you know and trust. I have always trusted Jacob."

"There's the paying for it that I don't like either." Conrad chuckled. "I don't want to pay for something if I can do it myself."

"I'm just not certain I can do it. I wouldn't want to get in trouble with the IRS!"

"What do you get when you remove the space between THE IRS?" Conrad smirked when Cora Mae frowned. "THEIRS." Conrad leaned forward and nodded. "As long as you remember that, you'll do just fine."

Cora Mae smiled. "I don't like to give my money away either. I think everyone feels that way. It's never a happy event. Speaking of events, — "

Conrad groaned. "You wanna talk about the egg thing?"

"Yes, the Eggs-Travaganza. You remember it's Saturday morning?"

"I remember."

"Well, the eggs aren't here yet and the candy comes tomorrow, so it'll be last minute crunch time for us to put this together. We're doing it the same as last year with some small changes. We're sectioning off an area for the little kids, so that they have a lower challenge area. I didn't like seeing the big kids stealing eggs from the small ones, so we're going to separate them a little bit."

"Sounds reasonable."

"And I told Amanda we needed to find a way to get the eggs back from the kids so we can lower the expense next year. I haven't worked those details all out yet."

"Wait, so you're going to let the kids find the eggs and then take the eggs away from them."

"Well, I don't think they really need all those eggs. I would think the mothers wouldn't want their house full of plastic eggs either, and buying two thousand eggs every year is an expense the City Council could cut too easily. I'm trying to protect the future Eggs-Travaganzas."

Conrad frowned in doubt.

"I've plotted it all out. You know about my pro and con lists. The pros just win out this time. I think the parents will prefer it, and the kids have short memories. Next year, they'll think it's the normal way to do it."

Conrad nodded. "I knew there had to be a list somewhere."

"Of course, but I don't know who is going to be the Easter bunny this year. Have you heard anything?"

"Oh, I didn't think about that," Conrad said. "I forgot Marvin moved away, didn't he?"

"Yes, and I haven't heard who they found for the replacement. I should have asked Saucy this morning. I saw him on the street when I was walking to Hart & Grace. He might have heard something. Cece Fields at the library always takes care of the Easter bunny because she has book readings with the bunny and a photo opportunity for the little kids in the afternoon. I'm sure she's found someone good. I can't imagine who it could be. Maybe Levi Nauchtman? He might make a good bunny."

"No," Conrad said. "His voice is too low. He'd scare all the little kids."

"What about your friend, Ned Carey?"

Conrad laughed. "I can see Ned pulling off Santa Claus, but I don't know if they make a bunny suit that would fit him. I'll be sure and mention to him that you thought of him though."

"Well, the Easter bunny could be female. Georgia Marks would be a good Easter bunny. Don't you think?" Cora said, as Jason approached the table with her lunch and a sack for Conrad.

"Chief, would you like me to get you a plate?"

Conrad nodded.

"Jason, don't you think your mother would be a good Easter bunny?" Cora asked.

Jason squinted his eyes and looked off through the window. "We need an Easter bunny for the Easter egg hunt at the park."

"Oh," Jason said. "I'm sure she'd be great at that."

"Have you heard who the Easter Bunny is going to be this year?"

"I haven't," Jason said. "I know Dorothy's been asking about that, too."

Cora looked at Conrad. "I think I better check with Cece and make sure she has found someone. We have lots of talent in this town, you know."

Conrad smiled. "The Easter bunny takes talent?"

"Well, of course. You have to love children, be kind, and patient—"

"Maybe you should be the Easter Bunny."

Cora Mae laughed. "I'm not going to volunteer, but I'm sure I can think of somebody to cast for that role."

Conrad gave her a dismissive wave. "I'm sure she will find somebody. Maybe she'll do it herself."

"That's a thought," Cora said. "Cece would be good at that. It's a really long day though. You have to spend the morning out at the Easter egg hunt and then the afternoon in the library and there's no pay, but that's why Spicetown is always so successful. The town thrives on volunteerism."

"Here you go, Chief." Jason slid a plate in front of Conrad and turned his coffee cup over to pour.

"No thanks, Jason. I'll just drink water."

"Okay." Jason walked away with the coffee pot in hand to warm up the customers at the other tables as Conrad watched wistfully.

"So, you are going to stop the coffee and give it a chance?" Cora said with a raised eyebrow.

"Yeah, I'm going to give it a try. If it would get rid of the heartburn I have, it would be worth it. If I try it and it doesn't work, then I'll have proof."

"So, you're trying to disprove your doctor?" Cora chuckled.

"In a way, yeah. I'm hoping he's wrong. I like my coffee. I'd hate to think it had turned against me this way."

"Conrad, there are other things to drink. You might try tea, or you could try decaf. There are other coffee substitutes that might fill the same need. If you had something to put in place of it, you might not miss it so much."

"We have decaf at the office. Maybe if I put my creamer in it, I won't notice. I do have to drink something."

"Just think how nice it would be if it was that simple."

"May be simple for you. I'd much rather take a pill." Conrad huffed.

"Oh, you don't mean that. If that's all you have to do is stop coffee to feel better, it will be one less thing you have to worry about." Cora looked out the front window of the café. "I've been watching the flower shop. Have you been in there lately?"

Cora pointed across the street. "They seem to still have a good business."

"I was in there about a month ago. They've got a young girl running it named Abby. She's not from the area. I'm guessing Herb Redding sent her down here to run the store until Hazel could come back."

"I was surprised they didn't close it when Hazel had to leave."

"Abby didn't seem to know anything about Hazel. I asked how Hazel was doing and she doesn't know her, so I'm guessing they just didn't want to lose the money they spent fixing the place up. As long as it can pay for itself, it made sense to send somebody down here to run it."

"Is she going to live in Hazel's house, too?" Hazel Redding had the first house on Cumin Court in the Redding subdivision.

"No. Hazel's house is all done now, but it's just sitting empty. Doug Keegan told me that they're going to make it a model house and they're letting people walk through it to show a sample of what they can build. They like to use those northern city contractors, so if you don't know any local folks to build for you, they'll write you a contract, and build you a house just like it."

"Is Miriam doing the same thing? Is she using the same contractor for all the houses that are going up in her subdivision next door?"

"No. Doug is selling the lots and the buyers are finding their own contractors. The one Jacob Hart has is the one that Miriam can't get along with. Doug Keegan did admit that the man is surly, so he and Miriam just knock heads."

"Why is Miriam Landry involved at all?"

"She's out there every day causing trouble of one kind or another. I don't think she has enough to do, but according to Gerald, Jacob asked them to keep an eye on his place because he's too busy at work right now, so Gerald and Miriam are going out there to meet with his contractor and oversee the day to day. Miriam claims that the contractor isn't doing the right thing and the contractor won't listen to her because he says he's got a contract with Jacob."

"Who nobody can find right now," Cora said.

"Exactly."

"He's probably just so busy. April 15th is just around the corner. Maybe he had to get away from everyone so he could finish up the work that he'd taken on."

Conrad leaned back in his chair and held his hands up. "What does Tim Grace do? He's working there, too, and he's building a house."

"But Tim Grace isn't a CPA like Jacob."

"Oh, I didn't know that," Conrad said. "I thought they were the same thing."

"No. Jacob hired Tim as an apprentice until Tim could get certified as a tax preparer, but he doesn't have an accounting degree. Jacob is certified with the State and he handles a lot of business records for local businesses, not just taxes. He does the

Fennel Street Bakery's books and Chervil Drugs. They have employee taxes to file and Jacob does all that for them. I'm not sure what Tim does throughout the year. He does do some simple tax preparation, but otherwise, he's just an assistant to Jacob."

Conrad scratched his chin. "Hmm, Well, he's got his name on the door."

"That's true," Cora said. "I don't know what their business arrangement is, but I know that's how it began."

Conrad glanced up and waved at a passer-by on the sidewalk outside. "It doesn't take much to be a tax preparer in Ohio. I don't think they are licensed or anything special."

"I like Tim and Tonya Grace. I just feel more comfortable having Jacob do my taxes. I know that he keeps things confidential and I just feel like I can trust him. I asked Amanda to find out from her parents who they use. I'm sure being self-employed is a lot more involved. She's already worrying about Bryan's taxes."

"Yeah, I hear that it's harder to do when you're self-employed. My taxes are easy."

"That's what Amanda says, and I just have my regular salary. Maybe I could do my own."

"Well, if you don't find Jacob soon, you may have to find out!"

Sheri Richey

CHAPTER 3

Tim glanced out the front windows of the shop and saw Gerald and Miriam Landry approaching. They were another irritant that Jacob brought into his life and he had no way to hide. He was certain Miriam had seen him through the front glass window.

"Good afternoon, Mr. Grace." Miriam slipped her handbag on her forearm and clasped her hands. "Is Jacob in the back?"

"No, ma'am," Tim said. "I haven't seen him today."

"Haven't seen him! Well, where could he be?"

Miriam's questions were always delivered with a hint of accusation and Tim looked down at his keyboard before shaking his head. "I'm sorry, I don't know. Perhaps he's out at the construction site. He wasn't here when I arrived."

"He's not out there," Miriam hissed.

"We checked over at the café," Gerald said. "I thought we might catch him having lunch, but no luck. If he comes in the office, could you ask him to call me? It's important and I haven't been able to reach him by phone either."

"Sure, Mr. Landry. I'll tell him you stopped by."

"Thank you. Come on, Miriam. We'll drive by his house and see if he's home." Gerald pulled open the glass door and ushered his wife out.

"Have a good day." Tim looked at the stack of work on his desk and smiled. Perhaps the afternoon would be productive.

§

"Hey, Chief. I'm sorry to bother you." Georgia Marks stood on one foot leaning against Conrad Harris' doorway. "Miriam Landry is in the lobby. She'd like to see you." Georgia's expression was apology enough.

"Okay, Georgie. Send her back." Conrad couldn't muster any enthusiasm. After motioning to Miriam to have a seat, Conrad sat down at his desk and looked at the doorway to see if Gerald might be following. Things always went a little smoother when Miriam's husband accompanied her. Seeing no help in sight, he clasped his hands on his desk.

"What can I do for you today, Miriam?"

"Conrad, we have looked for two days. We have been all over this town and Jacob Hart is missing."

"Now, Miriam. It could just be that he's out of town. He might have gone over to Paxton for meetings or to shop. Did you talk to Tim Grace?"

Miriam nodded curtly. "We've been there. Tim said he never came to work."

"Does he know what was on his schedule for today? I mean he may have had to be in court. I know Jacob testifies sometimes when there are court cases involving a business that he does the books for. He might have customers that he's seeing in neighboring towns. He might be fishing!" Conrad threw his hands up in the air. "When was the last time you talked to him?"

Miriam paused. "Wednesday, about ten o'clock in the morning. He called Gerald and I answered the phone."

"Okay, so what did he and Gerald talk about?"

"He's constantly worried about the house. That's why I was so upset yesterday. His contractor isn't following the instructions in the contract to mirror the house plans. The blueprints are supposed to be reversed and he asked for them to be printed that way but when the copies came in, they were the same as the original order, but his contractor said that wasn't a problem. He could just mirror them and build it the opposite way. He said there was no reason to delay starting work, but because of that, Jacob has been worrying about it.

"Yesterday was not the first time we've had a problem. The contractor keeps pretending like he's forgotten that the plans must be altered. He seems intent on building it the way the plans show it."

Conrad shook his head. "Well what exactly is involved in mirroring blueprints?"

"Exactly what I said, Conrad. The living room is on the left if you look on the plans, but Jacob wants it on the right. The kitchen is on the right and he wants it on the left. The whole thing has to be flipped."

"I guess I don't understand." Conrad continued shaking his head and trying not to roll his eyes. "If it's clearly stated in the contract, why is Jacob concerned?"

"I don't know. That has nothing to do with the problem, Conrad. The problem is that Jacob is missing. His car is not home, unless it's in his garage. We've banged on his doors. Gerald and I have been to his home twice."

"Was there any sign of a break-in? Anything out of the ordinary?"

"I think that is your department, not mine." Miriam huffed.

"Jacob lives alone?"

"Yes. He has a cleaning lady that comes once a week. She should have a key and you can go in and look around."

"Wait," Conrad said. "I'm not going to break in Jacob's house when he might just be visiting a friend or out of town for the day."

"Do you go off and not tell someone where you're going when you expect to be gone for the whole day?"

"Well, no, Miriam, but I'm in a little different position."

"Oh, you think there aren't people looking for Jacob? He has responsibilities, too. He would have told Tim Grace if he weren't coming in at all."

"Jacob is his own boss. He has his own business. It's only been a few hours—"

"Jacob has his own business, but he does have a partner." Miriam extended her hand and pointed toward Clove Street. "Would you not tell your partner if you're not going to be at work an entire day? Tim expected him to open the office today. He's never shown up and never called."

"Is Tim worried about him?"

"I don't know, Conrad. You need to call him and talk to him. Call his housekeeper. Find out if she knows anything. Maybe talk to his neighbors."

"Do you want to do this investigation for me, Miriam?"

"I want you to do your job, Conrad!"

"Okay. I will check into it." Miriam stood up, stiffened her shoulders, and walked out without a goodbye. Conrad recalled this was not Miriam's first time filing a missing person report. He hoped this time she was wrong.

§

"Mayor! How are you today?" Tim stood and motioned to a chair in front of his desk. "Have a seat. How can I help you?"

"Hello, Tim. I just popped over here to see if Jacob was in. I need to get my paperwork to him, and I keep missing him."

"He mentioned you just last week. I know he was expecting you to stop in. He's just been very busy these last few months."

"Oh, I can imagine. I'm sure it's very demanding to build a new home during your busy season. You and Tonya are doing the same, I hear."

"We are. She's very excited. She's getting a new space for her dance studio that's separate from the main house and that makes us both happy."

"I'm so glad to hear that."

"Yeah," Tim said. "It will be so peaceful. I won't miss having all the little kids tromping through my house to go to the basement when she has recital practice. The rehearsals seem endless." Tim rolled his eyes. "Now she'll be able to do that in her own building in our backyard and I'll be able to have peace and quiet in the house."

"That's wonderful," Cora said. "I'm sure Tonya will love having her own space, too. Well, when you see Jacob, please tell him to call me and I'll run my stuff right up to him. I know time is running short."

"Mayor, I'm happy to take your paperwork. I am—"

"Oh, I hate to leave it without talking to him first. We usually have a short meeting after he has looked things over."

"I understand, but it is rather late. If you change your mind, I'm happy to prepare your taxes for you. I can even look into advancing your refund if you'd like me to do that."

Cora Mae frowned. "Advance my refund?"

"Yeah, have you heard about that?"

"No. Is it some kind of expedited filing?"

"No, ma'am. We figure your taxes and we let you know what your refund will be. Then we give you your money up front. When your refund comes in, your refund is deposited in our accounts. Some people don't like to wait on their return money because they have plans for it."

"Oh, I see. No, I'm not interested in that. I can wait." Cora Mae smiled. "I'm just thrilled if I get a refund at all."

"I understand," Tim said. "But we can take a look and if you have the potential for a refund, we're happy to advance it for you."

"I've just never heard of that before," Cora said. "Jacob has never mentioned it to me. Is it a new thing?"

"No, it's been around for a few years. We run ads in the paper about it sometimes. A lot of folks think it's just easier to do it all at once, get it out of the way, and be done with it. They don't have to wonder when their refunds coming or how long it will be. They can just move on with their lives. Especially when you file late, sometimes the IRS gets behind, and it takes a while for them to process it."

"Well, that's awfully nice of you because that means you're out some money for a while. It's a very nice service for you to offer."

"We're happy to do that. You know there's only a few things in life you can count on, death and taxes, so we feel pretty confident that your tax money will show up and we're just trying to help."

Cora smiled and waved. "Thank you, Tim. I'll wait to hear from Jacob. Tell Tonya hello for me."

"Have a good day, ma'am."

§

"I'm back," Cora said as Amanda glanced up.

"Oh, good. I can run to the newspaper now and drop this off. Don't forget you have to go to mom's."

Cora jerked her shoulders. "Oh, you're right. I'd already forgot again. I have to get my hair done today. Why don't I just take the press release over to the newspaper on my way to your mom's shop? I can drop it off. It's just a block from the beauty shop. Then you won't have to get out."

"Is it still cold?"

"It's better now. The sun is warming things up. It's just that the wind is chilly."

"It looks like springtime!"

"Hmm," Cora hummed. "Looks can be deceiving."

Amanda handed Cora a file folder. "You can just drop it off at the front desk. They're expecting me to bring it by today."

Cora opened the folder and glanced at the copy. "This is lovely. Did you draw this?"

Amanda nodded shyly. "It's just a pencil drawing."

The ad was announcing the Saturday morning Eggs-Travaganza in the park and had a picture of the Easter Bunny holding a basket of eggs. "Mandy, you're very talented."

"Thank you," Amanda said. "I've been painting some small flowerpots. Bryan is going to have a booth in the park on Saturday. They're just the small clay pots, like I did last year."

"Those were lovely. Speaking of that, you mentioned before I left for lunch something about getting the eggs back."

"Oh yes!" Amanda said. "Well, I was thinking that rather than put the candy inside the eggs, we could use them as currency. When the children returned their eggs, they could pick out their prize. We could bag up the candy in different size bags and let the children pick the prize they want."

Cora looked at the ceiling in thought. "Egg currency! We let the kids use the eggs as currency."

"Exactly," Amanda said. "Although, I'm not sure candy will be enough. We could give them one piece of candy for each egg and count it out instead of putting it in bags. A lot of moms don't want their kids to have a bunch of candy."

"If we had gotten an earlier start, we could have ordered small toys or asked the community to donate. I bet some of the local businesses would be willing to give coupons and we could use those as well. Maybe 50% off a video game or a free movie rental from Chervil Drugs," Cora suggested.

"There's always ice cream or cookies from the bakery," Amanda added.

"That would be great. I'm sure they would be willing to do that and that would be better than giving a bag of candy."

"Oh, but there's not much time," Amanda said. "I don't know how we could ever get that together in just a few days. It's a shame we can't just go to the Chamber of Commerce."

Cora rolled her eyes. "But, of course, nobody can work with Miriam Landry on anything. I need to think about this. Maybe I'll make a list and see if I can make some calls tomorrow. We could get some donations, perhaps for the big prizes at least, because you're right, kids don't need all this candy. What do kids want?" Cora asked herself aloud. "They like video games. They like toys. They like movies, ice cream, ... Think about it, Amanda. Tomorrow we'll see if we can get a few donations, otherwise I think a piece of candy for each egg is a good way to go and then we're assured of getting all our eggs back."

Amanda nodded. "And maybe they'll even be in one piece!"

Cora Mae laughed as she waved and walked out of the office.

Sheri Richey

CHAPTER 4

"Hi ladies," Cora Mae said as she wrestled out of her coat and hung it on the hook near the door of Louise's Beauty Shop.

"Hi Mayor." Karen Goldman was in Louise's chair and Louise Morgan picked up a round brush to begin blow drying Karen's hair. Cora took a seat and pulled a notepad from her purse. During the drive over, she had been thinking about rewards for the children and needed to start her list. Arriving at the beauty shop early, Cora was surprised at how different the atmosphere seemed. She was usually a late afternoon customer and many times Louise worked her in at the end of her day. Most of the mid-day patrons were older and the atmosphere was quieter than it was at four o'clock. Louise switched off the hair dryer and grabbed a teasing comb, waving to Cora over her shoulder.

"How is City Hall today?" Louise said.

"Busy as usual. How has the beauty shop been today?"

Louise laughed. "Busy as usual."

"We're getting ready for the Eggs-Travaganza Easter egg hunt on Saturday. Amanda is making all the arrangements for the prizes."

"She loves doing that stuff. I'm sure she's having fun."

"Amanda is an invaluable asset to me. She's going to be at the Easter egg hunt with some of her flowerpots, too. She says she's been painting again."

"Oh, yes." Louise chuckled.

"I have a few in my windowsill. They're adorable. She's so creative," Karen said as Louise spun her around in her chair. Pulling off her cape, Louise handed Karen a hand mirror so she could look at the back of her hair.

"Short enough?"

"Yes. Thanks, Louise," Karen said as she slid out of the chair.

"You're welcome, hon." Louise began to sweep the hair around her chair and Cora Mae rose from her seat when a young girl beckoned her to the shampoo area. Returning with a towel on her head, she sat down in Louise's chair.

Louise begin combing through Cora Mae's hair as they looked at each other through the mirror. "So, is your Easter egg hunt this weekend?"

"Yes. It's Saturday morning. You should come out. Amanda will have her table with Bryan and it's so much fun to watch the kids."

"I'll be working Saturday morning, and after that, I just rest. I'm seriously thinking I need to cut down my hours a little. Five and a half days a week is a lot of standing. I'm getting old." Louise chuckled.

"I can understand that. Have you heard anyone say who the Easter Bunny is this year? You know Marvin Goddard always did it in the past, but he's moved away now."

Louise hummed. "I've heard some patrons talking about the egg hunt, but no mention of the bunny. No, I don't know. I thought you handled that."

"No. Cece Fields at the library always gets the Easter bunny because she uses him at the library after the hunt. They do a book reading for the young kids and then a picture opportunity."

"I haven't talked to Cece," Louise said shaking her head.

"Marvin has done it for so many years. I just realized this morning that she must have found someone new."

"I sure haven't heard anything."

"Well, have you heard anything about Jacob Hart?" All of the town's gossip filtered through Louise's Beauty Shop. It was a better source for news than the Spicetown Star.

Louise looked into the mirror and met Cora's eyes. "What's happened to Jacob Hart?"

"Oh, nothing. I just haven't been able to catch him. I thought maybe if he was out of town you might have heard. I've tried to call him and stop by his office. I just can't seem to connect with him."

"Wow," Louise said. "I took my taxes into him and he did them a couple of months ago, but I haven't talked to him or seen him since."

"Well, maybe I will catch him tomorrow. I know I've waited too late. I could kick myself," Cora said. "But now I'm getting in a pinch because time is running out."

"I'm sure you know he's building a house out on Miriam's land. That may be where he's spending some of his time," Louise said as she pumped the chair a little higher.

"Yes, I had heard that. Maybe the memories of his wife in the house that they'd lived in their whole life were overwhelming to him. Miriam probably convinced him that he needed a fresh start."

"Miriam probably pushed him into it." Louise scowled.

"The home he had with his wife was really big and maybe he doesn't want to have so much to take care of now. He might be thinking of retiring soon. I don't know what I'll do then," Cora said.

"I know," Louise said. "He does my taxes and Hymie's, too. I guess there's always Tim Grace, but I'm not sold on that idea yet. I've heard some sketchy stuff about him. I guess Miriam's subdivision is doing well?"

"It sounds like it. I think she's sold several lots. People like working with Doug Keegan."

"He seems like a nice young man," Louise said. "I heard Miriam's lots are cheaper and smaller than the Redding subdivision next door to it."

"I think Doug Keegan convinced Miriam that she needed to undercut what Redding was offering. If she offered a more affordable option, she could sell more that way."

"Good advice, I guess. I had a patron in here earlier this week that bought a lot on Cumin Court."

"It's nice to see all the growth in Spicetown," Cora said, smiling.

"As long as it brings in the right people," Louise said, snidely.

Cora had noticed that problems had increased in Spicetown along with the town's expansion. With the opening of the community center and new businesses, more people were moving to Spicetown for jobs and she hoped, for the wonderful quality of life Spicetown offered. With the good, sometimes came the bad.

"You know," Louise said, spinning Cora's chair to the left. "Annie Radford cleans house for Jacob Hart. You might want to give Annie a call and see if Jacob is out of town."

"I'll do that if I don't hear from him tomorrow."

"I guess he could be away visiting family. He has a son who lives near Philadelphia."

"An odd time for a trip though," Cora said. "I would expect his work to be very busy this week with the tax deadline looming."

"Every week is busy for us." Louise laughed when Cora nodded. "But everyone needs a break sometime."

"So true."

§

"Hey, Connie. Come on in."

Cora had one hand in an oven mitt and the other holding open the oven door as Conrad came through the kitchen door.

"Cora, you should keep your front door locked."

"I do," Cora said as she slid a pan of cheesy potato skins from the oven. "I heard you drive up and unlocked it."

"Hmm, okay. What can I do to help?" Conrad removed his duty belt and curled it into an extra chair before patting Cora's orange cat, Marmalade, on the head.

"You can get the drinks ready. There is coffee already made."

Conrad glanced at the coffee pot in conflict. "You know, I'm—"

"No, it's okay. No caffeine. The gingerbread creamer is in the mason jar over there."

"Well, maybe the creamer will help. Do you want iced tea?"

"Yes, please." Cora slid the potato skins onto a plate and took them to the table.

"I had another Miriam encounter today."

"Oh, you poor thing." Cora giggled.

"She can't find Jacob Hart. Did you ever hear from him today?"

"No, I didn't." Cora pulled out her chair and handed Conrad a bowl. "I've asked around and no one has seen him. Louise mentioned he might have gone to Philadelphia to see his son, but I can't believe he would vacation with the tax deadline so near."

"You were at the beauty shop today?"

"Yes. Louise uses Jacob for her taxes, too, but she filed early. I talked to Tim Grace, as well. He was expecting Jacob at work today."

"I didn't know about the son. I'll see if I can get contact information for him tomorrow. I've talked to his contractor and his house cleaner. Maybe something urgent came up with his son and he left unexpectedly."

"That might be. Otherwise I'm sure he would let someone know if he had been planning to go out of town."

"Miriam came in to file a missing person report. She claims he's disappeared, and he would never leave town without telling Gerald. I'm inclined to believe her. Jacob has Gerald keeping an eye on his construction project out there and it does seem odd he wouldn't tell him if he was going to be away."

"You think something bad has happened to him?" Cora dropped her spoon in her bowl and reached for the crackers.

"I don't know what to think yet. I'm meeting the housekeeper at his house in the morning. She's got a key and we're going to take a look inside."

"Annie has cleaned for him since his wife died. I think she just works a couple of days a week to supplement her retirement income. She goes to Jacob's church."

"You know her?" Conrad pulled a chair out from the table.

"Yes, she used to work for Dr. Mason years ago. I don't see her often, but she worked at the library book sale when they held it at the community center a couple of months ago, so I guess she volunteers for them."

"She seemed concerned when I talked to her on the phone today. She didn't know anything about Jacob being away."

"I hope nothing has happened to him."

"Are you going to try to do your own taxes this year?" Conrad smiled as he lifted his coffee cup.

"Do you think I can do it?" Cora cringed. "How long does it take?"

"I'm sure you can do it," Conrad said as he took a sip of coffee. "It takes me about half an hour, and I do it online. I'll send you a link."

"Tim Grace offered when I went in to see Jacob. He said he could give me a refund up front and then he'd file my taxes for me. Have you ever heard of that?"

"I've seen advertisements about advanced refunds. It sounds a little shady to me. I just don't trust them." Conrad shook his head.

"I don't feel comfortable with it either, but I'm just not sure I can do it. I might make a mess of it."

"You should give it a try."

"Maybe I will Sunday afternoon. I've got too much to do for the event Saturday. I can't worry about taxes right now."

"Okay," Conrad said. "But you've only got ten days left. What do you have to do for the egg hunt?"

"Amanda had some difficulty getting the eggs this year, but she's come up with a new plan that will require the kids to turn the eggs into us to get their prize. That way we can save the eggs and reuse them."

"Good idea. You may not get them all back though. What are the prizes?"

"We already had candy ordered but tomorrow we're going to try to get some local donations for bigger prizes. I feel like I'm a little out of touch. What do kids want nowadays?"

"They want to pet Briscoe." Conrad tapped his coffee cup. "This coffee is pretty good. What is it?"

"Briscoe? I never thought about that. That's a great idea. Would Briscoe be okay with that?"

"Do you want me to ask him?" Conrad laughed. "I'm sure he'd be fine with it."

"That could be a great prize for the older kids. A trip to the PD to meet Briscoe!"

"As long as I get a little warning before they show up, I can handle it. Now, what kind of coffee is this?"

"That gives me another idea! What about a visit to the Fire Department? Just a tour or maybe a chance to climb up into a fire truck. That sounds like fun."

Conrad nodded as he stood up to get more coffee.

"I still don't know who the Easter bunny is."

"No one at the beauty shop could tell you? I can't believe it." Conrad smiled as he slid back into his chair.

"I know. Shocking, isn't it? I'm beginning to think someone is trying to keep it a secret."

"They don't realize how much you like a challenge. Speaking of secrets, what kind of coffee is this? I may want to buy some."

"Oh, I don't know." Cora waved her hand dismissively. "It's something Bing used to drink when he wanted to avoid caffeine late at night."

Conrad tipped his cup forward and looked at his coffee. "How long have you had this around?" Cora Mae's husband, George "Bing" Bingham, had passed away over a decade ago.

"Oh, silly. It's not that old. I just picked it up. I don't remember what it's called. I'll get you some next time I'm out. What time are you meeting Annie tomorrow?"

"Eight o'clock. If he's not home, I'll start trying to find his son. Do you know his name?"

"Jeremiah."

Sheri Richey

CHAPTER 5

"Good morning, Amanda. What's all this?" Boxes were stacked around Amanda's office with a few in the lobby outside her door.

"They were here early waiting for us to open. I didn't expect so many boxes."

"Let's crack them open and see what we've got!" Cora tossed her coat into an empty chair and dropped her handbag as Amanda used her scissors to slice open a box near her desk.

"I'm almost certain we were only supposed to receive eight boxes. I can check the emailed invoice again, but I know we didn't have this much last year."

"Perhaps they are packaging it differently now." Cora frowned as Amanda pulled out a clear plastic bag full of small colorful toys. "Are you sure these boxes are for us?"

Amanda glanced at the box label. "It says Amanda Morgan, City Hall."

"Oh my. Do you think we've received two thousand toys instead of candy? We won't have time to wait on another delivery. Let's open another box."

"Toys," Amanda said as she handed the scissors to Cora.

Cora slashed at the tape on the top of a box and reached inside. "Candy!"

"Yay!" Amanda clapped her hands together.

Jimmy Kole peered around the doorframe with a furrowed brow. "I'm beginning to get worried about you two."

Cora Mae laughed and held up a bag of candy. "Our Easter supplies have arrived!"

"Where are you going to set up? I can have the guys move all this to the conference room or wherever you need."

"We aren't stuffing eggs this year." Cora lifted the box in front of her and then lifted one of Amanda's. "The candy is much heavier. Let's see how much we've got."

"Wait," Jimmy said holding up his hands. "What do you mean you're not stuffing eggs? What are you going to do with all this? Didn't you get your eggs?"

"Not yet, but they're coming. We're going to hide eggs and then when the kids turn them in, we're going to give them prizes." Amanda lifted each box and sorted them by weight.

"How many boxes did we get?" Cora looked around Jimmy and out into the lobby.

"Thirteen, so maybe we received our eight boxes of candy and then 5 boxes of toys." Amanda pointed her finger as she counted the boxes in the two stacks she'd made.

"Oh, that's an unlucky number." Jimmy scowled.

"I always forget how superstitious you are," Cora said. "It's actually a blessing because Amanda just came up with this great idea for us to get our eggs back, and now, we may have enough prizes to do it."

"Mayor?" Jimmy stepped aside when Laura, a deputy clerk who worked at the front desk, walked up. "There's a delivery man at the front door. He said he has a bunch of boxes for you?"

"Oh my," Cora said. "That must be the eggs."

"Laura, ask him to drive around to the back parking lot. I'll go out there and meet him," Jimmy said. Laura nodded as she left to deliver the message. "I can just load them in a truck and take them out to the city garage. Then they won't be in your way and the guys will have them for Saturday morning."

"Okay," Cora said, struggling with indecision. "Make sure the guys open the boxes and let me know that we've received the right thing. I'm feeling a little uncertain about surprise packages right now."

"I understand. Yes, I can open one and check before I take them out there." Jimmy turned toward the back hallway.

"Oh," Amanda yelled with her index finger in the air. "I need the invoices from the boxes, too."

"Gotcha," Jimmy said as he jogged off.

"Maybe I should go out there and check." Cora reached for her coat as Conrad Harris walked up to Amanda's office door and cleared his throat.

"Is it Christmas at Spicetown City Hall today?"

"Feels like it," Amanda said, smiling as she tossed the packing paper into her waste can.

"We received a surprise today. The eggs came early. They're out back with Jimmy and they sent some small toys along with our candy order." Cora dropped her coat back on the chair. She would let Jimmy take care of the eggs.

"Sounds like you're all set."

"Except for figuring out some rules," Cora said frowning at Amanda. "One piece of candy for one egg? And then we need to sort out these toys and put an egg count on each one. Oh, and I was going to call the Fire Chief—"

"It sounds like you still have a lot to do." Conrad held up his hand and backed away from the door.

"No, wait. Did you meet Annie this morning?" Cora walked around the boxes.

"I did."

Cora raised her eyebrows in question.

"We didn't find anything disturbed. Nothing suspicious. Annie did give me Jeremiah's phone number, so I'm going to give him a call next."

"If Jacob isn't there, you may alarm the boy."

"Annie said she didn't think they were very close. She said Jacob hadn't even seen his son since his wife died."

"Hmm," Cora said. "That's a shame."

"I'll let you both get back to work." Conrad held up both hands as he stepped backwards.

"Let me know if you find him," Cora called out as Conrad walked toward the front door and saw him wag his finger in the air to acknowledge her request. "The Chief gave me a good idea about prizes yesterday. He said the kids always want to pet Briscoe, so maybe we can offer that as one of the prizes. I was going to call the Fire Chief and see if he would entertain a visit to the fire station as one of the prizes, too."

"Great idea," Amanda said. "I thought about the shelter last night. You know Shelby Worth is having a bake sale at the Easter egg hunt to raise money for the shelter, but we could offer a free shelter adoption as a gift."

"With an adult's consent," Cora said, cautiously. "I don't want to get in the middle of a parental squabble that ends in a child's heartbreak."

"We can require they cash in their eggs with an adult present and then show the options to the parent first. If they don't want it offered, they can let us know." Amanda wrote a note to herself at her desk.

"Who is going to handle these transactions? You'll be busy at Bryan's table."

"Gloria from the community center has offered to help and I could ask Laura." Amanda pointed to the lobby.

"We need at least two people. How many vendors do we have?"

Amanda counted them off on her fingers. "Bryan; the Animal Shelter bake sale; the high school cheerleaders are selling candy bars and Spicetown spirit balloons; the Friends of the Library are doing a membership drive and Doug Keegan is setting up a table to display information about the subdivision lots. Five."

"I hope Miriam Landry isn't coming with Doug." Cora rolled her eyes.

"I think he's just bringing a small table to put out some pamphlets, just like the library is doing."

"I'm going to stroll down Fennel Street and see what I can collect. Dorothy Parish may be willing to donate something and I'm sure the bakery will want to be involved." Cora reached for her coat again.

"I'll do some inventory on these boxes to see what we have and start a prize list." Amanda grabbed a bag of toys and dropped it on her desk.

"A good plan. I'll be back soon."

§

"Jeremiah Hart?"
"Yeah this is Jeremiah. Who is this?"

"Good morning. This is Chief Harris of the Spicetown Police Department. If you have a minute, I was wondering if I could ask you a few questions."

"In Ohio?"

"Yes, sir." Conrad pondered whether there was another Spicetown. "Your father, Jacob Hart, lives here."

"Yeah, yeah. I'm just surprised. How can I help you?"

"I wanted to ask if you'd heard from your father recently or knew where he was. I've not been able to locate him, and he has friends that are concerned."

"Wow, no. I don't have any idea. I don't talk to my dad much."

"Do you know of any other friends or family who might have been in closer contact with him? Could he be visiting someone?"

"He never leaves Spicetown. He wouldn't even come to my wedding. I can't believe he's left town. All of his friends are right there, too. I don't have any answers for you. Sorry."

"Okay," Conrad said. "Thanks for your time." Conrad hung up the phone when he realized Jeremiah had disconnected the call. He hadn't even asked to be kept informed. His relationship with his father was more than remote. It was non-existent.

§

Cora crossed Paprika Parkway and headed down Fennel Street. She could have done this by telephone, but the weather was kind today and she was ready to get outside again. Glancing down Clove Street, Jacob Hart's SUV was not parked next to the building. Approaching Spicetown Blooms & Gifts gave her a brief pause, but she passed by to enter the Fennel Street Bakery first.

"Hi, Vicky. How are you?"

"Morning, Mayor. We're all doing well. What can I get for you today?"

Cora hesitated for a moment. "Just a cinnamon roll to go, Vicky. I was actually stopping in to see if you wanted to participate in the Easter Eggs-Travaganza on Saturday. We're giving away prizes to the kids this year and I thought you might want us to include a coupon from the bakery. Maybe a free cookie or something?"

"Oh, sure. You can put us down. I don't have any coupons made up, but—"

"That's okay. We'll make them for you. How many can you spare?" Cora handed her payment to Vicky for her roll and took the small white bag.

"We can do a dozen or so. Just let me know."

"Thanks, Vicky. I'll have Amanda email you. Thanks again."

"Sure thing. Have a good day."

Cora looked next door at the flower shop again. She hadn't been in there since Christmas and hadn't met the young woman running the store now. It wasn't normal for her to avoid any business, but she'd just been apprehensive after two failed attempts. The building seemed jinxed. Subconsciously, maybe she didn't want to know the new manager.

"Good morning." A petite brunette smiled from behind a glass counter. "Is there something I can help you with today?"

"Good morning," Cora said extending her hand. "I'm Cora Mae Bingham, the mayor of Spicetown. I'm sorry I haven't been in sooner to introduce myself to—"

"Mayor Bingham! It's so nice to meet you. My name is Abby and I'm the new manager. I just started the first of the year, but I've heard so much about you."

"You've moved to Spicetown?"

"I have," Abby said smiling. "It's such a nice little town. I was living in Columbus and there was so much crime. I was delighted when this opportunity came along."

"Well, I'm glad to hear you are happy here. The reason I stopped by is because the town is holding an Easter egg hunt this Saturday and we were hoping to offer local businesses an opportunity to donate to our prizes. Do you think your store would like to be involved? Maybe a coupon or a small gift that a child would like?" Cora wasn't certain this young girl had the authority to make these decisions. "There's no pressure to participate, but if you wanted to offer a coupon of some sort, we could—"

"I have just the most perfect thing!" Abby clapped her hands and bounced on her toes. "Give me just a moment." Holding up a finger, she disappeared through the curtains over the doorway to the backroom. Cora leaned an elbow on the counter and prepared to wait, but Abby popped back out from behind the curtain holding a giant cellophane wrapped rabbit wearing purple overalls and a straw hat. "Isn't it adorable? What do you think?"

Cora reached out to accept the rabbit as Abby held it out. "Yes, it's wonderful. Are you sure you want to give it away?"

"I'm sure. We ordered a few Easter decorations for the shop to include with flower gifts and this guy was just too big. We had him on display, but he took up the whole shelf and I had to move him to the back. I'd love to see him find a good home."

"Thank you," Cora said. "He's lovely and I'm sure all the children will do their very best to win him. You should come out and watch Saturday. The hunt starts at ten o'clock in the park."

"I know and we'll be there. I have a little girl who is very eager to attend. She's six years old."

"Wonderful! We'll put a tag on it to show it came from your shop and I'll see you there." Cora backed towards the door.

"Okay. I'm glad you stopped by. Come visit again soon."

Cora pulled the door shut behind her and sighed. The young woman had been very sweet and innocent. Perhaps this time, the store would not be clouded by despair.

"Good morning, Mayor. Are you Easter shopping?"

"Morning, Saucy. Isn't it a wonderful rabbit?" Cora held it out so Harvey Salzman could take a look. "The flower shop just donated it as a prize for the Easter egg hunt."

"You have prizes? I didn't know that. I just thought the kids found plastic eggs with candy in them."

"This year we're trying something different. Have you heard who the Easter bunny is going to be this year?"

"I, I don't know. I mean, I've not heard. Are you headed back to City Hall?"

"No, I'm going to cross the street and stop in to see if Dot is there. I wanted to talk with her before the lunch rush."

"Okie, dokie. I'll see you later," Saucy said as he glanced back to wave before walking down Fennel Street. Cora watched as Saucy waved at a friend across the street and strolled past the bakery. Stepping between the parked cars, Cora looked both ways and crossed Fennel Street with her purple bunny under her arm.

CHAPTER 6

"My oh my! You must have the Easter spirit!" Dorothy Parish leaned back and looked Cora Mae up and down before bursting out in laughter.

"You know I always embrace the holidays." Cora said with a playful smirk. "Actually, I'm here on a mission."

Dorothy pointed Cora to a chair and looked toward the counter. "Bring us some tea, please." Pulling out a chair to sit across from Cora, Dorothy took a deep breath. "Pray tell, what is your great Easter crusade?"

Leaning back, Cora paused for the wait staff to turn the cups upright and place the pots of hot water on the table. "We're trying something new this year at the Easter egg hunt, Dot. The kids will still hunt for eggs, but then they'll turn them in for prizes."

"No candy? That's un-American!" Dorothy laughed at her own joke.

"There will be candy as an option, but we also have small toys and some of the local businesses are providing coupons or giant purple bunnies to add to the prizes." Cora tapped the purple rabbit on the head that she had seated in the chair next to her. "I was stopping in to see if you wanted to include something from the café."

"Hmm, I don't have any coupons right now, but I do have some gift certificates. How about a free kid's meal or an ice cream sundae?"

"That sounds like a fantastic idea."

"Let me get them." Dorothy went behind the counter and Cora heard her holler at her husband, Frank. Dorothy had a boisterous personality and startled some people with her directness, but she had a good heart. Cora stirred some sugar into her tea and used her spoon to drop a piece of ice from the water glass into her cup to cool it.

"Here you go," Dorothy said sliding two envelopes onto the table. "I got you one of each."

"Thank you. I'm sure the parents will appreciate this as much as the kids. Are you coming out to watch the hunt?"

"No, I'll be working, but you can sure send everyone over here when they're done!"

"I missed you when I was in last. Jason told me you are delivering lunches out to the construction site every day now."

"Yeah, it's something I'm trying. We made some good money off those construction boys you had at the community center last fall. Since these workers are all in one spot, I thought it might pay off to give them some curbside service. Manual laborers are big eaters!"

"I think it's a great idea and I'm sure they appreciate it, too. Are you going to both subdivisions?"

"I am now," Dorothy said leaning forward on her elbow. "Miriam tried to run me off when it started, but the workers backed me. They said they'd walk over to the other subdivision to pick up their orders if they needed to do that. Miriam finally caved."

"I can't imagine why Miriam would want to prevent them from eating. That's crazy!" Every story Cora heard about Miriam Landry was worse than the last. "What was her reason for that?"

"It didn't have anything to do with the workers. She just didn't want me to benefit. Frank and I withdrew our Chamber of Commerce membership last year and didn't pay our renewal fees this year. Until there is a new president, we aren't interested." Dorothy sat back in her chair and crossed her arms over her chest. "The retail merchants in Spicetown deserve better."

"It's risky," Cora said, shaking her head as she stirred her tea. "She has a history of retaliating against those that don't comply."

"Yes, but she shouldn't be able to do that. I can't figure out how she gets re-elected. I think Gerald is paying people off to vote for her. I know I never have."

"Are there a lot of other business owners in town that have pulled out or is it just you?"

"Walter Mayfield at Sesame Subs withdrew before we did, but I don't know if anyone else left after. The Peppercorn Dry Cleaners wanted to leave. Almost everyone talks like they'd like to quit, but they're afraid of what Miriam will do to them."

"Maybe you should think about what you want as a retailer," Cora said as she took a sip of tea. "You could organize a merchant association and talk to the others about joining. I'm not sure what benefits you could offer, but—"

"Help with payroll taxes, financial planners, group health insurance, group discounts for wholesale orders," Dorothy said as she ticked the items off with her fingers. "There are lots of things we could do as a group. There is power in numbers. We don't get any of that stuff through the Chamber of Commerce. I told Miriam straight out, my membership fees get me nothing but you off my back and that's just not worth the fee anymore."

Cora couldn't stifle her laughter. She could visualize the entire confrontation and wished she had been there to see it. Miriam would raise her chin in the air and huff before walking away with an air that she was too superior to communicate with you. She'd done that to Cora many times. "Well, you know I have a rocky history with her as well, so I can't be of any help."

"How do I go about organizing something like that?" Dorothy scowled in deep thought.

"I'd start by searching the internet and seeing what other merchant associations offer. They're out there. That should give you an idea of where to start."

"My time is pretty limited," Dorothy said. "I feel like I live here sometimes. I might see if Jason is interested in helping. He could do some research for us. Kids know the internet better than I do. I told Georgia Marks that I'm thinking real hard about adopting that boy. He's a good kid and I sure do like having him around."

"He's a smart boy, too," Cora said. "He may enjoy the challenge."

"Good talking to you, Cora. I never get enough time to do that either. I'm glad you dropped by."

"Oh, Dot. I almost forgot. Have you heard who the Easter bunny is going to be this year?"

"I haven't heard a word on it. I know Marvin moved away. You don't know? I thought you arranged that." Dorothy pushed her chair under the table and held Cora's purple rabbit while she slipped on her coat.

"No, the library always coordinates everything because they use the volunteer up there. They own the rabbit suit."

"Ah, well I'll be. I'll keep my ears open and let you know if I hear anything."

"Thanks, Dot. And thanks again for the gift certificates. Tell Frank I said hello."

§

Conrad opened the blue cannister filled with Cora's fake coffee. She had sent him home with it after dinner and promised to find out the name of it the next time she went shopping. Frowning as he sniffed the grounds, he knew it wasn't normal decaffeinated coffee. There was something different about it, but he liked it. The more he drank, the less he missed his old coffee.

Conrad had one more call to make before taking Briscoe for his afternoon walk.

"Hart & Grace Tax Service. How may I help you?"

Conrad paused a moment, unsure who he was speaking to. "This is Chief Harris of the—"

"Oh, hey Chief! It's Tonya. Tonya Grace. How are you today?"

"Hi, Tonya. I'm fine. I didn't know Tim had put you to work up there."

"I'm just filling in during the afternoons a little so Tim can get something done while Jacob is out. I usually don't have dance class in the afternoons during the school year. Are you needing to get your taxes done?"

"No, I was actually calling about Jacob."

"Oh, everyone is looking for him. It's so weird for him to just disappear without notice. I can't imagine, uh, hold on a second, Chief."

Conrad heard the muffled words of Tonya telling Tim who she was talking to.

"Chief? Tim's here. Did you want to talk to him?"

"Yeah, if he can spare a minute."

"Hi, Chief. Were you calling to talk with Jacob?"

"I was following up on that. Several folks are telling me he's missing. When was the last time you saw him?"

"Ah, we don't always connect during the day. He's an early guy and I'm a night owl. I guess it was day before yesterday, maybe."

"And you don't know where he is."

"Nope, but he's not much of a communicator. He does his thing and I do mine. I'll sure let you know if he comes in though."

Conrad sensed that Tim wanted the conversation to end. "Do you know where he might have gone? You've worked with him for years. Surely you know each other pretty well. I'd appreciate any insight you might have."

"Our arrangement here is purely business, Chief. We aren't buddies. I do try to tell him if I'm going on vacation or something, but he's under no obligation to keep me informed."

"I understand, but this time of year I wouldn't think either of you would be considering a vacation. It's a busy time for you, isn't it?"

"Sure is," Tim said clearing his throat. "Are you needing to file your taxes, Chief? If you are, I'm happy to help out."

Conrad ignored the offer. "When you saw Jacob a few days ago, did you notice anything different? Did he come and go at a different time or did you sense anything off with him?"

"Nope, Chief. Same old guy. Sorry I can't be any more help."

"Well, you let me know if you think of anything or hear from him. Okay?"

"Sure will."

Conrad saw his call quickly disconnected and he frowned. How did two men end up partnering in a business when they didn't talk to each other? Jacob's new house was being built just a few doors down from Tim's. All outward appearances suggested they were close, yet Tim indicated they were two strangers passing each other mid-day. That relationship needed to be explored.

"Georgie?" Conrad slipped Briscoe's leash off the hook in the dispatch office and Briscoe climbed out from under the dispatch desk to stretch. "Did you get a chance to call the hospitals and the sheriff's office about Jacob Hart?"

"I did, Chief. He's not been admitted at any local hospital and the Sheriff's office doesn't have him listed on any report. Was his car at his house this morning?"

"No, it wasn't there. Go ahead and put out an APB on his vehicle."

"I'll get right on it, Chief."

"Thanks, Georgie. We're going out for a run."

Georgia nodded as she reached to answer the phone and Conrad headed down the long hallway to the side door.

"Come on, buddy. We'll check on your girlfriend and see if she's free." Doug Keegan's dog, Doozie, was Briscoe's best friend and she went to work with Doug occasionally, so the dogs had a chance to run in the vacant lots.

"I'm going to try to talk to Jacob's contractor. Maybe he's heard from Jacob. Hop in." Briscoe jumped into the driver's seat and stepped over the console. He preferred to ride shotgun and Conrad fastened Briscoe's harness to the safety belt.

§

"We're ready," Cora said. "Don't you think?"

"I hope so." Amanda tossed a broken plastic egg into the empty box. "Jimmy said all the eggs are loaded into the back of their trucks. He brought me all the invoices. They'll be out at the park at seven in the morning to start hiding them. I gave him the instructions we used last year to set up a soft fence line to keep the kids under six in the front area and the older kids can have the open space. I made two big signs with the prize options listed on them."

"Is Jimmy taking chairs out to the park with the tables? I think we forgot those one year."

"Yes, it's on the list of instructions now. I added another table and two chairs, so we'd have more room for the prizes." Amanda frowned. "Maybe we need tablecloths. We may want to put the prizes under the table out of sight."

"I'm sure there are some extras in the closet off the conference room." Cora pointed upstairs.

"I'll check and just throw them in my car. I should be out there early with Bryan setting up his plants."

"All the big prizes are labeled, and the coupons printed. Right?" Cora looked up to visualize her to-do list. "We need large bags to put the returned eggs in."

"Check," Amanda said as she looked at the list on her desk. "Did you ever find out who was going to be the Easter bunny?"

"No, I didn't, and I've asked several people. I tried to call Cece at the library this morning, but she was busy waiting on a customer. I asked the girl that answered the phone up there, but she didn't know either."

"Oh, Peggy Cochran called and she's going to be at the park offering free face painting. She said she might be a little late though because she has to wait on someone to show up to cover her at her store. The Carom Seed Craft Corner opens at nine."

"Wonderful! Now the only thing left to do is pray it doesn't rain again."

Sheri Richey

CHAPTER 7

Officer Fred Rucker jumped up from his chair in the dispatch booth as Conrad walked in. "Morning, Chief. You're in early for a Saturday."

"Yeah, but I needed someone out at the park early this morning and I knew it would be complicated right after shift change, so I thought I'd just come in myself." Conrad rubbed Briscoe's head as he unfastened the leash on Briscoe's harness.

"The park? Paprika Park?"

Conrad nodded. "The city is having the egg hunt this morning and they're going to be out there early hiding eggs. I want to get myself some coffee before I head down there." Conrad paused, remembering he couldn't make coffee.

Fred nodded and held up a finger as he reached to grab the phone. "Spicetown Police Department. Can I help you?"

Conrad walked into the break room and filled his pitcher with water. He could make the coffee

Cora gave him and hope he got through the morning without the real stuff. Strangely, he hadn't missed his coffee too much. It was inconvenient when he was out in restaurants and couldn't order coffee, but he was actually sleeping better and was feeling more alert. He'd gotten up this morning without using an alarm.

"Hey, Chief." Fred's head peeked around the break room doorway. "Phone for you. It's Doug Keegan."

"Okay, Fred. I'll be right there." Conrad walked down the hallway to his office and signaled Fred to transfer the call. "Good morning, Doug. How can I help you?"

"Sorry to call so early, Chief, but something went down out here a few days ago and I'm just finding out about it now."

"Not a problem. What's happened?"

"It looks like somebody drove a vehicle through the back of our building sites and tore up the area with tire tracks. I think they drove into the tree line, too. The trees that separate our lots from the Redding subdivision next door are damaged. I don't know if they wrecked out here or what."

"Do the tire tracks come from North Road?"

"No, they start in the empty lot next to Tim Grace's building site. It looks like someone jumped the curb on Lavender Lane and drove to the back of the lot into the trees. I wasn't out here yesterday, and the workers tell me that they saw it when they got on site that morning, but they just thought a delivery truck had done it. We didn't have any delivers that would have driven back to the tree line."

"Vandals, you think?"

"Maybe," Doug said. "I just thought I needed to let you know."

"I'll drive out and take a look. Are you out there now?"

"Yeah, I'm parked at the entrance, but Doozie and I are down here near Jacob Hart's building site. I'm waiting on the lumberyard to deliver his roofing shingles."

"Briscoe and I will be there shortly."

"Thanks, Chief."

Conrad waited for his coffee to finish brewing and went to get Briscoe. "Fred, I'm going to run out to Miriam Landry's subdivision and take a report. It sounds like they've had some vandalism or at least trespassing. Did Wink leave the camera here when he left?" Officer Harold Hobson was Conrad's right-hand man and he supervised the night shift patrol. Everyone called him "Wink" because he had one eye that didn't open all the way, but he told everyone that it was his good eye.

"Yeah, it's in the cabinet, but Wink hasn't clocked out yet. He's over on Celery Seed Lane taking a report on a break-in."

"After I take some pictures, I'll be at the park, if you need me."

"Okay, Chief."

Conrad looked down at Briscoe curled in the dog bed embarking on his first nap of the day. "You wanna go see Doozie?" Briscoe raised his eyebrows and jumped to his feet. "Come on, boy."

Doug Keegan's adopted shelter dog had bonded with Briscoe during their days at the Spicetown Animal Shelter and Conrad enjoyed getting them together when he could. When Doug was out at the new subdivision, he usually brought his dog, Doozie, with him so she could get some exercise. When the two were together, they were a team.

§

"Thank you so much, Rodney. I don't know what I would do without your help."

Rodney Maddox, a Spicetown Streets & Alley employee, flipped open the table legs to the long banquet tables and turned them over. "I'm happy to help, Mayor. You want them together?"

"Yes, please. I brought some tablecloths, so we can hide the prizes under the table. I've got a stand for Amanda's big sign and we can put that next to the table."

"It's not too cold today," Rodney said. "I was afraid it was going to rain again."

"Brr, I think it's pretty chilly." Cora wrapped her arms around herself. "It is supposed to warm up by mid-day, though. Rodney, have you seen the Easter bunny yet?"

"No. Who is the bunny this year?"

"I don't know, and no one will tell me." Cora Mae scowled. "It's a conspiracy!"

Rodney chuckled. "Maybe it will be a pleasant surprise."

Cora Mae nodded and then looked over her shoulder. "Is that Miriam Landry?"

Rodney glanced up quickly and away before Miriam could see him. "I don't think I've ever seen her at an egg hunt before."

"She's putting up a card table. Amanda would have told me if she'd registered to be a vendor. Doug Keegan was supposed to be here. Where is Amanda?"

Rodney pointed to Bryan's table where Amanda was lifting out small painted pots of different herbs.

"Is your wife coming out for the hunt?" Cora waved at Amanda when she caught her eye and she saw Amanda hand her box to Bryan to walk over to the main table.

"Yes, she's bringing Casey out. She's seven now, so she has to hunt on the big kid's side." Rodney opened the folding chairs and put them on the other side of the table. "Let me know if you need anything else. I'll be over by the truck, so just holler."

"Okay, thank you," Cora said, smiling and turned to greet Amanda.

"What's Miriam Landry doing here?" Amanda whispered to Cora.

"I was going to ask you the same thing!"

"Is she selling something?" Amanda frowned. "Maybe she's doing a membership drive for the Chamber of Commerce."

"At an Easter egg hunt? Oh my," Cora said shaking her head. "She must be desperate."

"No Easter bunny yet?" Amanda looked around at the volunteers with their shirts pulled out to create hammocks to carry the eggs.

"Not yet, but it's still early."

"Good morning, Mayor! Morning, Amanda." Peggy Cochran ran up with a tall stack of colorful wicker baskets. "I brought the shopping baskets I use at the store in case they were needed. Where should I put my painting table?" Peggy ran the Carom Seed Corner Craft store and aside from being an amazing seamstress, she had a special art for painting the little chubby cheeks of the children in Spicetown.

"You can set up right beside Bryan," Amanda said pointing.

"Oh, good." Peggy glanced over her shoulder. "I'd rather not be near Miriam. I don't think she likes children."

Cora nodded in acknowledgment. "What are you painting today?"

"I thought I'd make bunny noses and Easter egg cheeks. Where is the Easter bunny?"

"No sighting so far. Do you know who the bunny is this year?" Cora Mae cocked her head earnestly awaiting an answer. Peggy was close friends with

Cece Fields, who was the manager of the library, so Peggy surely knew the town secret.

"Hmm, I'm a little earlier than I thought, but luckily Sharon was free to cover for me at the store and she always comes in early. I don't know where the new bunny is, but I'm sure Marvin is thinking about us today. He has been the Easter bunny for close to twenty years now."

"You haven't heard who the bunny—"

"Hi there," Peggy said waving her hand in the air. "There's Abby from the flower store. I told her I'd be here today, and she has her little girl with her." Peggy scrunched up her shoulders. "I'm going to practice on her before the rest of the children arrive. See you later."

"Did you see that?" Cora Mae said to Amanda. "That's what happens every time I ask about the bunny. People dodge my question or run off without an answer. There's something fishy going on around here. You know Peggy has to know. She would have been the one to alter the suit for the new bunny and she's best friends with Cece. She's hiding it from me."

Amanda chuckled. "We'll surely find out soon enough, Mayor."

"Maybe the volunteers could use Peggy's baskets to carry their eggs while they're hiding them. Could you ask her if she'd lend them to us for a bit? Gloria is here now, and I need to help her get the prizes set up."

"Sure, Mayor."

"Good morning, Gloria," Cora Mae said as she walked around the banquet table. "I'm glad you're here early. Let me show you where the prizes are."

"Morning, Mayor. Amanda showed me the sign yesterday, so I know about the prize levels."

"Good. The prizes are under the table in these plastic bins. The candy is in the pink bin and Amanda labeled the others. The children can choose to take only candy if they prefer that. One piece per egg, or they can mix and match. They can take a prize worth ten eggs and then candy for the remainder."

"Gotcha." Gloria pulled out a chair and peered under the table.

"This big trash barrel behind you has a plastic liner in it and that's where you put the eggs that are turned in. Before the barrel gets completely full, we need to empty it into the back of the truck parked over there on the side." Cora pointed to a white truck with a city seal on the door and large lettering that said City of Spicetown Streets & Alleys.

"This is going to be fun," Gloria said. "Is it okay if I help hide the eggs?"

"Certainly, dear. Amanda is bringing some baskets and you can just go scoop some eggs up from the back of the truck."

Gloria clapped her hands softly as Amanda walked up with a stacked tower of brightly colored baskets and handed one to Gloria.

"I'll be right back, Mayor," Gloria said as she hurried off to find the egg truck.

"Where is that wabbit?" Cora scowled at Amanda as Amanda giggled.

§

"Now remember," Cece Fields said with her index finger pointed at the Easter bunny's head. "You don't talk. You nod your head. You shake your head. You clap your hands. You can even do a dance if you want to, but don't talk."

The Easter bunny held up a thumb in response.

"And do NOT take off your head! You'll scare the children right into therapy."

The Easter bunny nodded and offered a thumbs up in approval again.

"I'll be right here at eleven o'clock to pick you up. You'll get a lunch break and a chance to rest, then story time at the library at one o'clock followed by pictures. Okay?"

A final nod from the Easter bunny.

"Good luck," Cece said, as she held up her own thumb and smiled, as Spicetown's new Easter bunny waddled off towards the park entrance, lifting each foot extra high to keep from tripping over the giant furry feet.

Sheri Richey

CHAPTER 8

Conrad pulled his car over in front of Jacob Hart's lot and saw Doug Keegan standing in the front doorway.

"Hey, Chief." Doug jumped down onto a plywood sheet that was being used as a sidewalk. "Sorry to drag you out here again, but I thought you'd want to see this."

Conrad nodded and walked up to meet Doug with Briscoe at his side.

"It's back here," Doug said pointing to the standing tree line that separated the two subdivisions. "See these tire tracks that start at the curb?"

Conrad had noticed them when he had parked his car. It looked as though someone had driven through Tim Grace's front lawn that did not yet have grass and exited onto the paved road. "I think they exited at the curb."

"They go all the way back to the trees and then to Tim's house. Someone must have been out here messing around. You can tell which way they were going?"

"Yeah, you can tell from the puddle by the edge of the street. Vehicles push and pull water through the puddles. Let's walk out there," Conrad said pointing. "Where's Doozie?" Doug Keegan's slick-coated dog was running across the street to join them and Briscoe was whining for Conrad to give him permission to say hi. "Go on." Conrad waved his hand at Briscoe with a smiling smirk as Briscoe barked a thank you. The two dogs danced ahead as the men stepped gingerly over the moist earth.

"I guess this was all out here yesterday, but I didn't know about it until today. It must have happened night before last."

"I know the night patrol comes out here," Conrad said. "Wink has them drive through both subdivisions. He hasn't reported any disturbances. Maybe it was kids, horsing around. Anything missing?"

"Not that I know of. There's not much out here except some material piles but they're all pretty heavy. The Miller's house is under lock now and the Lester's house just has sheetrock stacked inside. No tools to take. The Grace's house just has some scrap wood around."

"Looks like Briscoe wants me to take a look." Conrad pointed ahead at the trees where Briscoe was perched. Doozie was bouncing all around him trying to interest him a playful romp, but Briscoe was all business. "What's up, buddy?" Conrad scratched Briscoe's head and bent forward to look closely at the brush around the base of the trees. Briscoe turned, poking his nose at a clump of bushes with tiny buds sprouting on the tips of its twigs as Conrad's glance swiveled from left to right. "There's something in there? I don't see anything."

Doug looked over Conrad's shoulder as he pulled back the sprouting twigs. "I don't see anything."

"Go play," Conrad said with a wave of his hand and Briscoe galloped out into the yard with Doozie. "I don't know. Must be nothing." Conrad turned around and pointed. "It looks to me like a truck or SUV drove from the house to the tree line and then jumped the curb when they left."

"You can tell it was a truck?" Doug looked down at the tracks.

"Yeah, truck tires, but I'm going to take some pictures. You may find out later that something is missing."

"Good idea," Doug said as his head jerked around at the sound of the delivery truck turning into the subdivision. "It looks like the roofing shingles are here. I need to go wave them down."

"Go ahead," Conrad said with a nod. "I'm just going to look around. I'll keep an eye on the dogs."

§

Rodney Maddox leaned against the tailgate of the city truck and dipped his plastic basket into the pool of pastel-colored eggs. Before leaving the city garage, the guys had opened all the boxes and dumped mounds of Easter eggs into the truck bed and secured a tarp over the top. Picking out the ones that had popped open, he added another handful to the basket to help the volunteers hide the eggs.

"Hey there, Mr. Easter Bunny." Rodney laughed when a giant furry Easter bunny tugged at his arm. "You are a mister, aren't you? You sure--"

The costumed bunny clasped Rodney's upper arm with both hands and pulled him toward him. With a wave of his hand beckoning Rodney to follow, he hurried toward the rhododendron bushes that fronted the street edge of the park.

"What? Where are we going?" Rodney followed and looked back over his shoulder before putting his basket of eggs on the ground. "What's over here?"

The bunny stopped and bounced on his toes as he pointed between the thick bushes. A man's body was sprawled with his face turned away and Rodney shook the man's shoulder.

"Are you hurt? Hey, buddy?" Rodney removed his hand quickly and gasped. "Stay here. I'll go get help."

"Mayor, is the Chief here?"

"No. Are you okay? You—" Cora reached out and put her hand on Rodney's arm.

"No. There's a body over there," Rodney whispered leaning toward Cora. "Shh, in the bushes. I think he's dead. We need the Chief."

"A body?" Cora said, but barely any sound escaped. "Let me call him."

Cora quickly dialed the police department and told Officer Fred Rucker that they needed assistance. Rodney rocked back and forth on his feet.

"Is he coming?"

"Yes, someone is coming right now. Rodney, you need to sit down over here. Who is it? Do you know them?"

"I think it's Mr. Hart. Sorry, I'm a little freaked out right now. I should probably go back—"

"Wait. Did anyone else see it? Where is he?"

"Over by the bushes back behind the truck. The Easter bunny found it and came to get me."

"The Easter bunny!" Cora lowered her voice when she saw others glance her way. "Who is the Easter bunny?"

"I don't know. He just pulled me over there and I told him to stay there. I should go back."

"Here comes Wink. He's running across the street now. You can show him."

"Morning, Mayor." Officer Harold Hobson nodded to Cora and then glanced around at the vendors and volunteers milling about. "Fred said you called?"

"Yes, Wink. Rodney here will show you." When Rodney didn't move, Cora tapped his arm. "Rodney?"

"Yes, ma'am. Sorry." Rodney's face was pale, and he took a deep breath.

"Show Wink where he is."

"Oh, yes ma'am. This way."

Cora looked around before casually following along behind Wink. She didn't want his uniformed presence to cause alarm, but everyone seemed very occupied with setting up tables and unpacking items. The volunteers with egg baskets were closely studying the shrubs and flowers as they searched for the perfect hiding place and Cora felt she could safely slip away. The egg hunters had not started to arrive yet.

As Rodney pointed, Wink crouched down and pulled the bushes back for a closer look. Cora peered over his shoulder and knew immediately that the body belonged to Jacob Hart.

"Should I call an ambulance?" When Cora looked down the length of Jacob's body, she saw the awkward position of his legs and his neck was at an exaggerated angle. "Maybe I should call the coroner."

Rodney took several steps back and looked toward the city truck.

"Rodney, what happened to the Easter bunny?" Cora walked around the tall bushes and glanced across the park. Someone large, white, and furry would certainly stand out. "I don't see him anywhere."

"I don't know, Mayor. I told him to stay here and that I would go get help."

"You don't know who he was?"

"No," Rodney said shaking his head. "I don't even know if it was a man. He didn't say anything. He just pulled me over here and pointed. He didn't kill Mr. Hart, did he?" Rodney's breath became rapid as his eyes widened.

"No. No, I'm sure he didn't. This didn't just happen." Wink stood up and pulled his cell phone from his pocket.

"Rodney, you don't have to stay here. You can go sit down somewhere and rest or hide some eggs if you'd prefer. Just don't talk about this to anyone. You look like you're in shock. You need to take it easy for a minute." Cora turned Rodney away from the bushes and guided him around the tall shrubs to the city truck. "Wink will take care of this."

"I'm sorry, Mayor," Rodney whispered. "I've just never seen a dead body before. I touched it. It was an accident. I didn't know. I didn't mean to mess anything up. I thought it was some guy sleeping. I touched his shoulder."

Cora squeezed his arm. "It's okay, Rodney. Relax. You didn't do anything wrong. Take a deep breath." Cora's phone buzzed and she glanced at the screen. "The Chief is on his way."

Sheri Richey

CHAPTER 9

After saying goodbye to Doug Keegan, Conrad held the door open for Briscoe to jump in. "Sorry, buddy, but we've got to go." Conrad clipped Briscoe's harness to the safety strap and pulled his own seat belt on before starting the car. "Fred says we've got a dead body in Paprika Park, so we need to go check it out." Conrad ruffled the back of Briscoe's neck as he pulled his squad car out onto North Road. "I hope it's not the Easter bunny. Cora Mae will... Let's just say, it won't be good."

Briscoe sat up focused on the road ahead and ready to work as Conrad tapped the console in his car to call Wink.

"Hey, Chief," Wink said. "You on your way?"

"Yeah, I'm coming in from North Road. Where are you?"

"We're over behind the bushes that go across the front—"

Conrad heard Cora Mae in the background. "The rhododendrons. The southeast corner."

"The Mayor says they're rhodo—"

"Yeah, I heard," Conrad said. "You and the mayor there? Did you call the coroner yet?"

"Fred called it in, and they said to just bring them the body, so he called an ambulance. I'm pretty sure the body was dumped here. There's a bullet wound but no blood."

"The quicker we can remove the body, the better. A bunch of people are going to be showing up soon. Who knows about this?"

"The mayor said Rodney Maddox told her and he said the Easter bunny told him. I guess that's all that knows so far."

"The Easter bunny!" Conrad barked. "Who's the Easter bunny?"

"That's just the thing, Chief. Nobody knows and now I can't find him."

"You can't find a giant white rabbit? I'll be there in a minute."

Coasting slowly into town, Conrad saw an ambulance parked inconspicuously at the side entrance to the park, away from the planned event. Pulling into the police station, Conrad decided it would be better to walk over to the park. The egg hunt was scheduled to start in forty minutes, and he didn't need to add to the chaos. Fastening a leash onto Briscoe's harness, they strolled leisurely across the street and away from the main entrance. Despite his attempt to look casual, Briscoe pulled hard against his lead and led Conrad toward the bushes.

"Chief?"

Conrad's head snapped back when he heard a female voice call to him from the street.

"Chief, can I talk to you a minute?"

Conrad saw a small blue sedan pulled over to the curb and Cece Fields, Spicetown's library manager, was waving her hand out of the window with a large furry friend in the passenger seat.

"Morning, Cece." Conrad nodded. "I'm in a bit of a rush, but I think your friend here can help." Conrad looked into the eyes of the furry Easter bunny head and frowned. "Saucy, is that you in there?"

"Yeah, Chief. I found that body and I got Rodney to go tell the mayor."

"Can you take off your head and tell me about it?" Conrad glanced at Briscoe who sat calmly beside the car showing no concern about the bunny costume.

"Chief, I told him not to talk to anyone and not to take his head off. I didn't want any of the kids to see him. It's my fault, but I didn't want to ruin the Easter egg hunt."

"I understand," Conrad said nodding. "Well, I need to get over there. Did you see anyone around the body? How did you find it?"

"Nobody was around, Chief. I was just wandering, and I thought I saw something yellow under the bush. There shouldn't be any Easter eggs that far over and I went to make sure nobody had hidden one over there. That's when I saw him."

"You go do your Easter thing, Saucy, and come to the station when you're free. I'll get your statement then." Conrad waited for Saucy to nod his large furry head. "Cece, please don't talk to anyone about this."

"Oh, I wouldn't, Chief. I promise."

Conrad stepped back and waved as Briscoe began pulling him down the sidewalk. Giving in to Briscoe's urgency, Conrad jogged behind him. "Find Wink."

§

Cora watched the emergency technicians push the stretcher away with Jacob Hart's body firmly secured and covered. It was a relief to see they had been successful at addressing the issue without alerting everyone near the main park entrance.

"I agree with Wink," Conrad said. "The lividity shows Jacob died on his back, probably from a gunshot wound. I'm not a medical examiner, but I can tell that much. It looks like somebody dumped him here."

"How awful," Cora said sighing. "I can't imagine why anyone would want to kill Jacob. He was a quiet man, kept to himself most of the time."

Conrad looked at Wink. "We need to find the crime scene."

Wink nodded and then turned away to tap his shoulder microphone to report to dispatch that the body had been removed.

"Any reports of gunshot recently?" Conrad looked down as Briscoe sniffed the area where Jacob's body had been.

"Not on my shift," Wink said. "I can check the reports though."

"You do that," Conrad said as he patted Briscoe's back. "I need to run back out to the subdivision and finish up what I was doing. If the Easter bunny comes into the station, we need to get a statement from him."

Wink chuckled.

"Did you talk to the Easter bunny?" Cora said grabbing Conrad's arm. "Who is it?"

"Yeah, I did. I told him to go do his bunny thing and then come by the station." Conrad laughed.

"Who is it?" Cora asked again.

"You'll find out. I don't want to ruin the surprise."

"Conrad!" Cora scolded as Briscoe followed Conrad around the rhododendrons to the street.

§

"Isn't it too cold to plant things?" Miriam Landry peered over the banquet tables lined with small pots of herbs as Amanda Morgan stretched across the table to arrange them.

"Not at all, Mrs. Landry. Most plants tolerate cool temperatures well as long as it isn't below freezing." Bryan Stotlar pushed an empty box under the table and lifted another into his chair.

"These small pots are meant for indoors. Some people like to cook with fresh herbs and it's an easy way to keep them handy."

"Hmm," Miriam said feigning interest. "I'm not much about cooking, but I guess you have to do something once the Christmas tree season ends."

Bryan Stotlar ran Stotlar's Nursery on the north edge of town across the street from Miriam Landry's new subdivision. His business had been annexed last year and was now within the Spicetown city limits. Before opening the nursery, Bryan's primary business had been managing a Christmas tree farm and he provided all of Spicetown with fresh trees for the holidays.

"The nursery is actually a full-time business," Amanda said to Miriam. "Bryan also does landscape work and is very busy with the new housing project."

"Yes, well," Miriam said with raised eyebrows. "Have you joined the Chamber of Commerce yet, Mr. Stotlar? Your business is within the city limits now and Chamber membership offers a number of benefits."

"Uh, no. I haven't, but I'll be sure and look into that." Bryan lifted a peace lily from the box in his chair and sat it on the corner of the table.

"Here you go," Miriam said as she thrust a folded pamphlet in front of Bryan. "The application is on the back along with a coupon for payment."

"Thank you," Bryan said, nodding. "I'll take a look."

Miriam sighed heavily and then moved to the next vendor table.

"So, that's what she's doing over there." Amanda scowled. "She didn't sign up to be a vendor. Doug was supposed to be here for the subdivision, and he didn't show."

"What benefits?" Bryan pushed the empty box under the table and sat down. "I didn't know there were any benefits to being in the Chamber." Bryan opened the pamphlet.

"The only benefit I know about is that once you're a member, Miriam quits bothering you. I think that's why most people join." Amanda chuckled. "It's like paying for protection."

"Is she pushing the Chamber or the subdivision? I thought she was setting up the table to try to sell those lots. She never lets Doug Keegan do his job." Bryan sat back in his lawn chair and crossed his ankle over his knee.

"Hi, kids. What's the old bat doing here?" Dorothy Parish walked up to the corner of Bryan's plant table and tilted her head toward Miriam. "Did she just come out to try to ruin everyone's holiday fun?"

"She's trying to get Bryan to join the Chamber," Amanda said.

"Don't do it, honey. It's a racket," Dorothy said. "Frank and I got out of that last year. We got tired of paying dues for nothing."

"I was just asking Amanda what the benefits were. I don't know of any," Bryan said with a shrug. "She gave me this brochure."

Dorothy took the pamphlet and opened it. "This says community support and discounts. A bunch of vague stuff. She doesn't offer anything. And this says group insurance plans! That's a flat lie. Me and Frank have been talking about starting a merchant's association."

"That sounds like a great idea," Amanda said.

"I talked to the mayor about it. If we all get together, I think we can help each other. It doesn't matter whether it's an old business, like mine, or a new one, like yours. If we all promote each other, we all benefit. Where is Cora Mae?" Dorothy looked around the park at all the volunteers. "Is she hiding eggs?"

"She was here a minute ago," Amanda said.

"She's probably chasing that Easter bunny." Dorothy laughed. "Did she find out who it was yet?"

"I don't think so," Amanda said. "I haven't seen the bunny yet."

"Well, I'll leave these with you, then." Dorothy handed two envelopes to Amanda. "I gave Cora a couple of gift certificates for your egg prizes, but Frank thought I ought to bring over a couple more."

"Thank you," Amanda said. "I'll give them to her as soon as I see her."

"I need to get back to the café. We're having a meeting about this merchant association," Dorothy said pointing at Bryan. "Do you think you might be interested?"

"Yeah. I'd like to hear more about it." Bryan nodded. "I'm always looking for a way to work with other businesses."

"I'll talk to the mayor and see what information I can find. Maybe some of the other towns around us have already done it," Amanda said.

"Good idea." Dorothy waved. "See you kids later."

Amanda glanced behind her and saw Dorothy walking toward Fennel Street. "Where is the mayor?" Amanda frowned at Bryan. "And the Easter bunny? People are going to be showing up soon."

Bryan shrugged. "Maybe she's got the bunny cornered."

Sheri Richey

CHAPTER 10

"These are so lovely." Tonya Grace held a small painted pot filled with rosemary to her nose.

"Thank you," Amanda Morgan said.

"I bought one last year in that essential oil store that used to be on Fennel Street. It was basil and I use it all the time, but I love the smell of rosemary."

"There are several different ones here on the table that are rosemary," Amanda said, lifting the plants to show the different designs.

"I may just have to have another one!"

"Spring is in the air!" Cora Mae announced as she walked up beside Tonya at the Stotlar Nursery table. "I'm so glad the sun has come out today. No more dreadful rain. How are you, dear?"

"I'm great, Mayor. It's looks like the kids are having a blast." Tonya looked over in the fenced area where the small children collected eggs, most with their parents following closely behind them. "I saw the big prize sign at the entrance. I wish I would have known. I would have offered a free dance lesson."

"That's a fabulous idea!" Cora held her arms out. "I can't believe we didn't think of that. Amanda and I were searching our brains for ideas at the last minute. There's still time to add your name to the list. Don't you think, Amanda?"

"Sure. I've got markers in my purse. Would you like me to add it?" Amanda began digging in her handbag.

"Please do," Tonya said. "A free dance lesson, winner's choice!"

"We'll certainly do that, and we won't forget you next year. We're hoping this new system works well. I hate to see the kids disappointed, but I think a lot of parents would prefer they not get quite so much candy. Is Tim with you?"

"No. He's out at the house. You know we're building in the new subdivision and it's very time consuming. We have to run out there almost every day."

"Yes, he told me," Cora said. "I was in his office looking for Jacob. I just can't seem to catch him in."

Tonya laughed. "He's building, too. They're both running back and forth every day. Jacob's house is just a couple of lots from ours."

"I need to drive out there and look around," Cora said. "I haven't been out there lately."

"You might find Jacob out there easier than you would going by the office!" Tonya laughed. "Bye, ladies."

Cora glanced warily at Amanda as Tonya walked toward the next table.

Amanda's eyebrows raised at Cora's expression.

"That's odd. Everything I've been told has been quite the contrary." Cora tilted her head.

"You would think she would know," Amanda said.

"Yes," Cora said, shaking her head. Leaning closer, Cora pointed at Amanda with her schoolteacher index finger. "Now, where is that Easter bunny?"

§

"Twice in one day," Conrad said as he glanced over at Briscoe who was riding shotgun in the front seat of the squad car. "Don't get used to this now." Conrad chuckled. "It's not just about play time. We've got work to do. I need to find out when Jacob Hart last came out to his new house to look around."

Conrad waved as the delivery truck from the lumberyard passed him near the subdivision entrance. He should be able to catch Doug Keegan before he left. Pulling over to the curb behind Doug's truck, he saw Doozie running across the empty lots toward Doug.

"Hey, Chief. I was just about to head out of here."

"I'm glad I caught you. Do you have a minute?" Conrad motioned to Briscoe to jump out of the car and they walked toward Jacob Hart's lot. The ground was soft from the previous rain, and Conrad could see where the delivery truck had driven around the side of the construction.

"Sure. I'm not in a hurry to get anywhere. Miriam decided to go to the Easter egg hunt this morning, so I could come out here."

"I was wondering if you could give me some contact information for each of these houses. I need to see if I can find anyone that's seen Jacob Hart recently."

"I can make you a list and drop it by the station if you want," Doug said.

"Thanks," Conrad said. "With the workers coming and going, it may be hard to talk to all of them. There's a lot of activity out here during the day."

"Yeah, but Jacob was never out here when there was work going on. He told me he was going to let Gerald Landry oversee things because he had too much to do with tax season. A lot of the owners come out in the evening and check on things, but I don't think Jacob even did that every day. I only saw him a couple of times and that's been weeks ago. Gerald was out here one evening checking on Jacob's house when I was leaving for the day. I think it was Thursday. He probably kept in touch daily with him."

"Was Miriam with Gerald Thursday night?"

"I didn't see her, but she might have been inside the house." Doug shrugged. "I thought Gerald was just checking out the day's progress."

"What about Tim Grace? Does he come out during the day or just after work?"

"He's out here pretty much every day and evenings, too. His wife comes once in a while. He's very involved in the daily construction. I guess his workload isn't as heavy."

"Maybe not," Conrad said. "I'm told he has different clients. Jacob works with businesses and Tim more with individuals, I think."

"Tim talked to me about doing my taxes for me. I need to take care of that. I was going to try doing it myself, but then Redding Realty didn't send me a W-2." Doug huffed and shook his head. "I'm not asking them for it either. I don't need any problems."

"Did Tim tell you what you have to do?"

"He said he could take care of it. I'm going to take my stuff up to his office on Monday."

"Where's Briscoe?" Conrad saw Doozie standing in the empty lot on the other side of Jacob Hart's house, but Briscoe wasn't with her. Conrad whistled and turned when he heard Briscoe bark. "What's he doing up there? I better go see."

"Okay, see ya, Chief. I'll bring that list by."

"Okay, thanks." Conrad waved as Doug helped Doozie into the truck and trudged up the soft incline to the tree line at the back of the lot. "You better not be chasing rabbits again!" The last time Briscoe had run through the thicket behind the subdivision barking was when he had discovered a nest of baby rabbits. Conrad had talked him down from harming them that time, but Briscoe was in a frenzy about something again.

"What is it, boy?" Conrad walked under the low-hanging branches and pulled back a bush to see Briscoe standing near an oak tree several feet in. The wooded area was about twenty feet deep, and Conrad could see the construction sites in progress on Cumin Court in the subdivision next door owned by Redding Realty between the bare twigs. Once the trees bloomed out, this thicket would provide privacy between the homes.

As he drew closer to Briscoe, he knew why he had been drawn to this spot. The forest floor was covered in dark wet leaves from the recent rainfall, except for a large strip where the vegetation had been disturbed. The earthy scent of the woods changed to a metallic smell as he grew closer.

"Fred?" Conrad barked into his cell phone as soon as Officer Rucker answered. "Who's on today?"

"Hey, Chief. Tabor is here in the office and Asher's out on patrol."

"Send Tabor out to Lavender Lane. I'm out here now and I could use some help. Did Wink go home?"

"Not yet. He's in the break room writing up a report from this morning, but he's off the clock."

"Okay, thanks. Let me know if the coroner's office calls."

"Sure thing, Chief."

Conrad pocketed his phone and motioned to Briscoe to come to him. Squatting down, he wrapped his arms around Briscoe's neck and patted his side, as Briscoe panted with an open mouth. "I think you found our crime scene, buddy."

Sheri Richey

CHAPTER 11

"I don't wanna." The young man stomped his foot and looked up at his mother. "I want the ice cream."

Gloria smiled and tried to feign a chuckle. "Well, there are toys to choose from, too. Maybe we should take a look at those."

"Perhaps we gave them too many choices," Cora whispered to Amanda.

"We'll be better prepared next year." Amanda pointed to a young girl in the fenced area reserved for the children under six. "See the little girl with the pink coat on? She wants that purple rabbit so bad. She keeps counting and when she finds out she doesn't have enough eggs to get it, she goes back to work. I wish we had more than one of those. She'll be heartbroken if someone else gets it first."

"Gloria seems to be handling this okay." Cora frowned when the little boy won the argument with his mother and grabbed for the ice cream gift certificate from Gloria's hand. The argument continued as they walked away because the boy wanted the ice cream right now and it wasn't even lunch time yet.

"Better than I would." Amanda huffed.

Cora looked around the park. "I was surprised to see Tonya Grace at your table earlier."

"They don't have any kids, do they?"

"No. Tonya always wanted children though." Cora Mae knew how that felt. She and Bing had never been blessed with children despite wishing for them all those years.

"Have you figured out who the Easter bunny is yet?" Amanda smiled.

"I've got an idea, but the bunny won't talk!"

Amanda laughed.

"Every time I get close and look into those eyes, he runs off. I haven't heard him say a word all morning. He just makes hand gestures and hops around, nervous as a cat."

"I thought maybe it was Mr. Salzman," Amanda said shrugging. "Only because he hasn't stopped by. He usually shows up to watch the hunt."

"I thought the same thing and I think I could tell if I could see in those eye holes." Cora Mae frowned in frustration and Amanda giggled.

"He's doing a good job, whoever he is."

"Hey, Mayor. I'm back if you need me." Rodney Maddox walked through the iron gate of the entrance to the park. "I just gave my statement to Wink."

"Was the Chief over there?" Cora asked.

"Nah, I think Fred said he went out to Lavender Lane."

Cora Mae nodded as Rodney walked away.

"Statement?" Amanda whispered. "Did something happen?"

"Yes, but I've not been given permission to discuss it yet." Cora looked sideways at Amanda.

"Oh, okay. Is everybody okay?"

"No, indeed they are not." Cora straightened her shoulders and gave a curt nod.

Amanda's eyes widened in concern.

"I'll tell you all about it Monday," Cora said as she squeezed Amanda's arm. "Today, we chase down that bunny rabbit!" Cora punched the air in a show of confidence and marched off towards the giant white rabbit.

§

"Fred?" Conrad hollered toward dispatch as he walked out of the break room with a pitcher of water. "Can you do a little research for me today?"

"Yeah, sure."

"Can you run a report search and pull anything you find on Jacob Hart or Hart & Grace Tax Service? I need to look over any cases you find."

"I'm on it." Fred gave a thumbs up sign.

"Oh, and I need a search warrant on Jacob Hart's home and office, too. You can tell Asher to put that in when he gets to the office." The police station was eerily empty. Officer Asher was on patrol and the other available officers were out on Lavender Lane.

After pouring the water in his coffeemaker and measuring out Cora's coffee, he tipped the blue container at an angle and saw it was running low. As much as he hated to admit it, he hadn't suffered from heartburn this week. He pulled out his phone and sent a quick text to Cora to remind her he needed to know the name of the coffee so he could pick up more.

Sliding a notepad across his desk, he made a list of people he needed to contact. Jacob Hart only had one family member to notify, and that needed to be done first. Then he would look for the housekeeper and Jacob's business partner, Tim Grace. He was not looking forward to dealing with Miriam Landry at all, but he needed to reach out to any friends that might have known Jacob well.

Conrad poured coffee in his cup and reached for the phone.

"Jeremiah Hart?"

"Yeah."

"This is Police Chief Harris again, from Spicetown. We spoke a few--"

"Yeah, sorry I can't help you."

"I understand, but actually I was calling to let you know that we did find your father, Jacob Hart, this morning."

"Oh, good. Great. Thanks for letting me—"

"I'm sorry to have to tell you this, but your father's body was found. He died from what appears to be a gunshot wound, but we can't say definitively until the coroner completes her examination."

"What? Wait. He's dead? Where did you find him?"

"In Paprika Park this morning."

"Somebody shot him in the park? Wow, Spicetown sure has gone downhill since I left."

"No, we believe his body was moved there," Conrad said. "Do you know anyone who would want to hurt your father? Was he in any dispute with anyone?"

"I don't know. I don't know anything about what goes on with him anymore. I told you, we're not close."

"When did you see him last?"

"I don't remember. Look, I gotta go. Thanks for calling—"

"Will you be coming to town soon?" Conrad heard voices in the background. "I may need to speak with you again. I don't want to keep you, but—"

"You can give me a call next week if you need to. I'll probably just do everything from here. Sorry, but I gotta go."

"Okay. We'll be in touch."

Conrad heard the call reception end from the absence of background noises. Ordinarily he would have asked the local police to handle the death notification, but he sensed from his earlier conversation with Jeremiah that he wasn't going to have any difficulty with the news.

Glancing over at Briscoe curled up on his dog bed, Conrad smirked. "I guess I could have saved some time and just sent him a text message."

§

"Tim, have you been out at the house this morning?" Tonya Grace sat in her car on Lavender Lane with the heat running. She had driven out to their new construction after visiting the Easter egg hunt, expecting her husband, Tim, would be out there.

"Nah, not yet. Where are you?"

"I'm out at the house now. I thought you'd be here. Did you know there is crime scene tape at the back of Jacob's lot and the empty lot between us? The police are up there now."

"What? No, it wasn't there yesterday. What are they doing?"

"I can't tell. There are two police cars out here, but I can't see much."

"Well, don't worry about it as long as they're not on our land. Do you want to go over to Paxton and get some lunch? Then we can go look at those lights you wanted."

"Okay. I'll be home shortly."

Tonya jumped as someone knocked on her car window when she disconnected her call. Looking in her rearview mirror, she saw another police car had pulled up behind her while she had been on the phone.

Clutching her chest, she rolled down her car window. "Chief, you startled me."

"So sorry," Conrad chuckled. "I didn't mean to sneak up on you."

"I was on the phone and not paying any attention. What's going on out there?" Tonya pointed toward the back of Jacob's house.

"We're just out here checking on a few things. Seems somebody drove their truck through the mud and back into the tree line." Conrad pointed in front of Tonya's car. "See the tracks on the road here. They cut through your lot."

Tonya peered over the steering wheel. "Oh, no. Tim will not be happy about that."

"Where is Tim?" Conrad glanced toward the house.

"I just called him and he's home. I thought he'd be out here, so that's why I stopped by. I was out at the Easter egg hunt."

Conrad nodded. "When was the last time you were out here?"

"Oh, earlier in the week. Tuesday maybe? I ran out to check with the contractor on something because Tim couldn't get away from work."

"So, you guys didn't know about the joy rider who drove through your yard?"

"I didn't, and Tim hasn't mentioned it. He was out here yesterday, I think. I'll ask him."

"Tell him I will need to talk to him sometime this weekend. If you would, just ask him to stop by the station when he can."

"I will, Chief. We're running over to Paxton this afternoon, but I'm sure he'll be happy to stop by."

"Thank you." Conrad tapped the top of her car before stepping back. "You have a good day."

CHAPTER 12

"Hi, Cora Mae. How did the egg hunt go?" Dorothy Parish stood at Cora's table in the Caraway Café with an order pad in one hand and her other hand propped on her hip. "Did you work up an appetite?"

"Hey, Dot. I heard you stopped by. I wish you could have stayed. The kids had such fun."

"Did you ever catch that Easter bunny?"

Cora Mae threw back her head and laughed. "Whoever it is, they can hop faster than I can."

Dorothy chuckled. "I guess the mystery continues. Huh?"

"We'll get to the bottom of it," Cora assured her with a stern shake of her head. "Now, what's the special?"

"Chicken and dumplings." Dorothy tapped her order pad with her pen.

"That's exactly what I wanted." Cora smiled.

"Coming right up."

Cora glanced at her phone and saw a text from Conrad about coffee and a later text saying he had spoken with Jacob's son. He was going to be interviewing all day. She had been released from her vow of secrecy.

Dorothy returned with a small pitcher of hot water for tea and Cora motioned for her to join her.

"Dorothy, when was the last time you saw Jacob Hart come in?"

"Are you still looking for him? It's been a few days. I think Wednesday. I remember we had the shrimp salad on special and Jacob doesn't like shrimp. That man is a meat and potato guy." Dorothy smiled. "Miriam Landry came in looking for him, too. Has Jacob left town?"

Cora leaned forward and spoke softly. "Dorothy, Jacob is dead. They found his body this morning."

"Dead?" Dorothy covered her mouth and looked around. "What happened?"

"Well, we don't know all the details yet, but it would be nice if we could retrace his steps this week. I know you've been running meals out to the construction site every day. Have you ever seen him out there?"

"No, never. I've seen Tim Grace once or twice, but never Jacob. I don't think he ever left work during the day except to come over here for a late lunch. He opened around ten each morning and came by here after one o'clock."

"Was he usually alone?"

"Always," Dorothy said. "He was all business during the day. Even when it wasn't tax season, he still seemed busy."

"So, Tim didn't lunch with him."

"Nah, I rarely see Tim Grace. Once in a great while Tonya might drag Tim over here for lunch. I don't think Tim and Jacob got along that well anymore, but Jacob doesn't talk about it."

"I wonder why they stayed in business together if they didn't click," Cora said. "I don't think they're partners. It was Jacob's business to start with, so surely they could have gone their separate ways if it wasn't working out."

"I think in the beginning, Tim helped Jacob. They seemed to work on accounts together. Now I think they keep their clients separate." Dorothy pointed to the kitchen. "Frank says Tim can't be trusted. I don't know why, but Frank and his brother, Ted, won't use Tim Grace for anything. Jacob handled all the accounts for Chervil Drugs, but Ted wouldn't deal with Tim."

"Hmm, I wonder what happened." Cora glanced toward the kitchen to see if she could catch Frank's eye.

"Whatever it was, it happened a long time ago. Maybe back when Tim helped Jacob with his accounts. I don't know. It could just be a personal issue. I just know Ted feels strongly about it and Frank agreed with him."

"Ask him for me when you get a chance," Cora said. "Okay?"

"Sure thing. Now let me go grab your dumplings." Dorothy slid from her chair and pushed through the kitchen door as Cora pulled a notebook from her handbag. Her memory was just not what it once was.

"You know Annie Radford, don't you?" Dorothy said when she returned with Cora's plate of chicken and dumplings.

Cora nodded.

"She might be able to tell you something about Jacob. She cleans for him, but I think they were pretty good friends. Annie used to be close to Jacob's wife, so she's kept an eye on Jacob since Margie passed away. Annie has had a hard time with her son getting into trouble. Jacob always tried to help her out. When that boy got arrested a few years ago, Jacob got him a lawyer because Annie couldn't afford it."

"Where is Annie's son now?" Cora stirred sugar into her hot tea.

"I think he lives with her. He was in jail for a short time, but he didn't get sent to prison, thanks to Jacob. I don't think he's worth much. He's probably just mooching off Annie."

"That's a shame," Cora said. "What was he arrested for?"

"Attempted murder. He got in a bar fight and hurt some guy really bad, but Jacob's lawyer got the charge reduced to battery and he was released pretty quick."

"I'm sure he was grateful for Jacob's help."

"Nope, not a bit," Dorothy said, shifting her weight to her other hip. "That no-good thug told Jacob he didn't want his help."

"What? Why in the world would he act like that?"

"Jacob told him he wasn't doing it for him. He was doing it for Annie because for some crazy reason she cared what happened to him. It got pretty heated apparently. Jacob told me the kid never gave Annie anything but grief."

"Jacob told you about this?"

"Oh, yeah," Dorothy said, sliding into the chair across from Cora to let a couple move down the aisle between the tables. "He said Quentin had come into his office that morning right after he got released from jail and told him to stay out of his business. He was still mad about it when he came over for lunch. Ungrateful little--"

"That's horrible. I can't imagine why he would react that way when someone was trying to help him."

"Do you know Quentin?" Dorothy rolled her eyes. "He's always been a jerk."

"I knew him when he was a young boy, as a student." Cora Mae had taught fifth grade at Peppermint Elementary for over twenty years before becoming mayor, so she knew everyone in town when they were ten years old. "He was an assertive child, but I haven't seen him in years."

"I'm sure you don't hang out in the same places." Dorothy laughed. "I bet the Chief knows him. You ask him."

"I will. Thank you, Dot. If you think of anything else, please let me know or call the Chief."

"Okay, Cora, but you be sure and let me know when you find out what happened to Jacob. Whatever it was, he didn't deserve it." Dorothy pointed a finger at Cora before hurrying off to the window to grab the next order.

§

Cora pulled into the parking lot of the Spicetown Police Department and parked beside Conrad's car. She had taken an order of chicken and dumplings to go when leaving the Caraway Café and had stopped by the Sweet & Sour Spice Shop to pick up Conrad's coffee. She hadn't been certain he would be in the office but knew he wouldn't have taken time to eat. He never did when he had a case.

Struggling to pull open the glass door with two bags in her hand, Officer Asher ran up behind her.

"Hey, Mayor. Let me get that for you."

"Thank you, Roy. You have perfect timing."

"Happy to help, ma'am. That sure smells good." Roy Asher took a deep breath.

"I would have picked you up lunch, Roy, if I'd known you were here. I was just over at the café and they have chicken and dumplings on special today. I thought the Chief probably needed lunch. He's having a busy day."

"Yes, ma'am." Roy said as he stepped inside behind her. "I thank you, but I just had lunch. It still smells mighty good though. The Chief's in his office. He might be on the phone, but I'm sure he won't mind if you go on in."

"Thank you, Roy."

Cora walked into Conrad's office as he nodded at her. While he continued his phone conversation, she opened the bag of coffee and poured it into the blue cannister she had given him and took off her coat. Shoving the empty package into her handbag, she took Conrad's lunch into the break room to warm it up in the microwave. Officer Asher was filling a large thermal cup with coffee.

"Any news on Jacob yet? Has the coroner called?"

"Not as far as I know," Asher said. "I think they found the place he was killed though. Chief found a place out behind Jacob's new house and it looks like it probably happened there. We have to wait on forensics to know for sure."

127

"He was shot out there and someone brought him to town? If Jacob was on his own land, why move him?"

"I know. Crazy, right? I wouldn't want to be moving no dead body around." Roy chuckled. "Shooting somebody is easy, but nobody wants to touch it after."

"Hmm," Cora said after the microwave timer beeped. "That's true. There must have been a good reason to go to all that trouble."

Walking back into Conrad's office, Cora opened the steaming container and placed it across from Conrad.

"What's this neighbor's name again?" Conrad leaned forward and breathed in heavily, mouthing a silent thank you to Cora. "How long has he lived there?" Conrad scratched notes on his notepad and Cora leaned forward to glance down, but the notes were in a language no one else could read. Conrad's handwriting was indecipherable to mere mortals.

"Okay. I'll meet you there in the morning and I'll see if I can talk to Mr. Decker after I look through the house. Thanks, Annie."

Conrad hung up his phone and pushed his notepad aside to pull the food closer. "This smells wonderful. You've been to the Caraway?"

"Yes, I just had lunch there and this was on special."

"Thank you. I'm starving. I didn't get down to the bakery this morning, so I didn't get breakfast either."

"Are you still going to the bakery for coffee with Ned and the guys?" Cora gave him a scolding frown. "I thought you weren't drinking coffee."

"Oh, I'm not. I make some here and take it with me, but I do usually get a little something to go with it." Conrad patted his stomach. "I can't give up everything at once."

Cora smiled. "Well, your coffee tin is filled now. Has the Easter bunny been by yet?"

Conrad raised an eyebrow and smiled.

"Well, he has to give a statement, doesn't he?" Cora held out her hands and shrugged.

"Yes, but unfortunately you just missed him."

"Who is the Easter bunny?" Cora leaned forward in her chair and glared at Conrad until he laughed.

"Now, you don't want me to just tell you, do you? Where's the fun in that?"

"Conrad, if you don't tell me, I'm going right up to the library to snatch that big furry head right off of him."

Conrad snorted when he laughed with his mouth full. "Simmer down." Conrad held his hands up with his palms out. "I'll give you a hint."

Cora sat up straight and nodded.

"It's your favorite senior citizen who—"

"I knew it was Saucy! That little old man must be worn out from running from me all morning." Cora squeezed her hand into a fist.

"You were chasing the Easter bunny?" Conrad said with a scolding shake of his head.

"I knew if I could get a good look in those eyes, I could tell. Amanda and I thought it was Saucy. He always comes out to watch and he hadn't shown up. I'm going to bend his ear when I see him. Keeping secrets from me..."

"Now, it's not his fault. Cece told him to keep his head on and not talk to anyone. She wasn't trying to pull anything over on you. She just wanted to maintain the mystery for the children."

"Oh, that's a bunch of hooey. She was trying to keep it from me, too. Cece was one of my best students and now she's gotten sneaky as a cat. I'll be having a talk with her, too."

"Okay. Okay," Conrad said, waving his hands and smiling.

"Now tell me what Annie said."

"She's going to let me in the house tomorrow morning. I'm hoping to find some clues in there about what was going on in Jacob's life. No one seems to know much about him. Annie is telling me he had a feud going on with his neighbor, Joe Decker. He apparently didn't get along well with Tim Grace either, which surprised me. Other than that, I can't find any enemies. Maybe it was an accident somebody is trying to cover up."

"Well, I talked to Dorothy at the café. She said Jacob always had lunch there every day but hasn't been in since Wednesday. When do you think he was killed?"

"Alice hasn't called yet, but it's been a few days I'd guess. The crime scene wasn't fresh."

Cora Mae grimaced and waved her hand in front of her face. She didn't want the details of that. "Alice may not work on Saturdays." Alice Warner was the county coroner and had an office in Paxton.

Conrad nodded.

"Dorothy also told me that Jacob had a quarrel with Quentin Radford, Annie's son. Seems he helped Annie get an attorney when Quentin was charged with attempted murder a few years back. The lawyer got the charge reduced and Quentin didn't appreciate it. Dorothy said Quentin went up to Jacob's office when he got out of jail and told Jacob to mind his own business."

"Hmm," Conrad dabbed a napkin on his mouth. "I remember that. He got in a bar fight and beat the living daylights out of Clyde Schofield. I thought he was gone for good that time."

"So, you know Quentin?"

"Oh, yeah. Worthless. Asher's picked him up before out at the Wasabi Women's Dance Club. He's a mean drinker. He's also been arrested for burglary several times. He's done some short state time, but I thought with his record, they'd send him to prison for what he did to Clyde."

"They might have if Jacob hadn't helped him. I can't believe he was so ungrateful." Cora frowned and sat back in the chair across from Conrad's desk.

"I'll ask her about that in the morning. Maybe she can explain it. There must have been something more there."

"Have you talked to the Landrys yet?" Cora furrowed her brow in sympathy.

"Not yet. I'm saving that for tomorrow. I'm hoping Miriam's temperament is better on a Sunday."

Cora Mae laughed. "I wouldn't count on it."

CHAPTER 13

"Thank you for meeting me, Annie. I appreciate it." Conrad pulled Jacob's front door closed and locked it with the key.

"Keep the key, Chief. I don't have any need to get back inside and I don't want Jeremiah accusing me of anything. Did I tell you I called that boy yesterday?"

"No, but I called him as well. I guess you probably know the young man pretty well."

"Since he was knee high to a grasshopper. The boy is just angry. I've never understood it. I called him last night to tell him I was sorry about his dad and to ask him when he was coming to town. He said he's too busy."

"Yes, he told me the same."

"There are things that boy needs to take care of! Jacob's house, his business, his new house out there in that subdivision half built. He's got to make some decisions. Not to mention a proper burial and service."

"Did you tell him this?" Conrad raised an eyebrow.

"You're darn right I did. He didn't even know his dad was building a new house. He said he'd just put the houses up for sale and close the business. He acted like he could just push a button and it was done. He never even mentioned a service. I told him the pastor at the church would help him out. He just needed to call him."

"The coroner's office will contact him about that when they are ready to release Jacob. I guess he doesn't have to come home if he doesn't want to." Conrad shrugged.

"Everybody thinks my son is trouble, but I can tell you one thing. My boy will make sure my things are taken care of when the time comes."

"Did your son and Jacob ever mend their ways? I know Quentin was angry with Jacob a few years back." Conrad pocketed the house key and walked down the front steps.

"Nah, that was a misunderstanding. Quentin thought Jacob was taking advantage of me and there ain't nothing further from the truth. Jacob was a good man, but Quentin tends to think the worst of people."

"Did they have any more run-ins after he got out of jail? Did they ever see each other?"

"Nah," Annie said shaking her head. "Quentin didn't like me working for Jacob. He complained about it some, but he and Jacob didn't ever talk again. I told Quentin to stay out of it."

"Well, I'm going to go next door here and see if Mr. Decker is home. If you think of anything, Annie, please give me a call." Conrad handed her a business card and tipped his hat to her as she walked back to her car.

Walking down to the sidewalk to go around the fence separating Jacob's house from the Decker property, Conrad looked for the front walkway. Hidden in high grass, he saw small oval steppingstones that led to the front door. The Decker house was noticeably in need of paint and the front picture window appeared to be covered with a bed sheet decorated with yellow roses.

Conrad knocked on the aluminum screen door and then opened that door to knock on the wood entry door. Just as he released the screen door to abandon his attempts, the wood door opened a few inches.

"Mr. Decker? Joe Decker?"

A man in a dingy undershirt peered out at Conrad with a scowl.

"I'm Chief Harris. I was looking for Joe Decker. Is that you?"

"Yeah," the man growled. "What do you want?"

"Good morning. I'm sorry to bother you, but I wanted to ask you a few questions if you have a minute. It's about your neighbor, Jacob Hart."

"What about him?" The door opened slightly wider and Conrad could see the interior of the house was dark, but the television was on. The smell of fried bacon wafted through the opening along with the scent of a damp musty cellar.

"Mr. Hart has passed away and we are trying to determine when he was last seen and contact his close friends."

"Ah ha!" Joe Decker yelled before breaking into a big smile. "Well, I'm not one of them."

"Can you tell me when you saw him last?" Conrad pulled a small notebook from his chest pocket.

"I don't know. It's been cold. I don't get out when it's cold and I don't see him unless he comes over here complaining."

"You don't notice when he leaves or comes home?"

"Nah. I don't pay him any mind. Never have. He's the one worrying about me all the time."

"I don't know what you mean," Conrad said with a furrowed brow. Annie had mentioned that Jacob quarreled with his neighbor, Joe, over the noise Joe made in his shed.

"He came over here when I was working in my shop and told me to quiet down. I haven't ever gone over there and bothered him at all. He wasn't very neighborly, so I just ignored him."

"Do you notice when he has visitors or when he leaves his home?"

"I told you I don't pay him no mind. I don't snoop on my neighbors. Not my business."

"I'm not asking you to snoop," Conrad said sternly. He didn't have the patience he needed for this conversation today. "I'm asking you a direct question. Mr. Decker, when was the last time you saw Mr. Hart?"

Joe Decker paused and took a half step back. "Wednesday, no Thursday night," Joe said with a grunt. "He came home and left again right before dark. That's all I know."

"Thank—"

The door closed in Conrad's face. "Nice talking to you," Conrad muttered to himself.

As he turned to walk back to his car parked on the street in front of Jacob's house, he saw a woman sitting on a porch swing across the street. She didn't smile or beckon to him, but she didn't run inside either, so maybe that was a sign.

Sauntering up the walk, Conrad tipped his hat. "Good morning, I'm Chief Harris. I don't believe we've ever met."

"No, I'm Polly Jeffers and I try to stay out of trouble." The young woman smiled while kicking her bare feet back and forth to rock the swing slightly.

"Do you live here?"

"I do. I live here with my husband, Scott. He took over Dr. Ingles' practice on Tarragon Street."

"Ah, the new eye doctor! Yes, I heard old Doc Ingles retired."

"It's not really new now. We've been here two years. Moved here from Paxton. Scott worked for a franchise clinic there, but he wanted his own shop. I don't know why. It's twice the work, but it makes him happy."

"Well, we're glad to have you. I was just wondering if you know your neighbor across the street at all?" Conrad removed his hat and stepped up on the porch.

"Have a seat. Sure, we know Jacob. He was real helpful when we first moved in. I haven't seen him in a couple of days. Are you looking for him?"

"When did you see him last? Do you remember?" Conrad lowered himself into a white rocking chair and leaned forward on his knees.

"I don't know. He comes and goes to work. It's been too chilly to sit outside much lately, so I just see him if he drives up when I'm getting the mail or coming and going myself."

"His car is not in the garage," Conrad said. "I was hoping you knew when he left."

"I haven't been out here very long. My husband just dropped me off after church. He had to go back and help out at the church for a bit and I'm just waiting on him to get back so we can have lunch."

"His neighbor, Mr. Decker," Conrad said, pointing to the house he had just visited, "said he thought he saw him come home from work Wednesday or Thursday and then leave shortly after that. He hasn't seen him since."

"Hmm, that old curmudgeon might be keeping an eye on all of us. Maybe he's right." Polly shrugged her shoulders. "I was here Wednesday, but I didn't notice him come and go. Seems like I saw him earlier in the week arguing with some guy in his driveway. I was in the living room and thought I heard voices, so I peeked out the curtains. I saw Jacob and another guy yelling at each other. I don't know many people in Spicetown though, so I have no idea who it was." Polly slipped her feet back into her shoes.

"Can you describe him?"

"His back was to me. He was taller than Jacob, seemed younger and had blonde hair, but I just saw the back of his head."

"What about a car? Was the guy's car out front?"

"Uh, I didn't notice. I only looked for a minute. I can ask Scottie when he comes home. He looked out, too. He might remember."

"Did Mr. Hart get many visitors?"

"No," Polly said with a furrowed brow and then titled her head. "Is something wrong? Is Jacob missing?"

"No, Mr. Hart's body was found yesterday. We're trying to trace his steps the last few days and determine—"

"He's dead? Jacob is dead?" Polly put both feet down on the porch to stop the sway of the swing.

"Yes, ma'am. I'm trying to trace his movements the last few days. Is there anyone you know that I might need to speak with? Any other neighbors that might have seen him?"

"He has a lady that comes to help him with the house. She's not there every day though."

"Yes, I've spoken to her." Conrad said standing and pulling out a business card. "If you think of anything, please give me a call. I'll try to catch your husband later. I appreciate your help and it was nice meeting you."

"You, too, Chief." Polly waved as Conrad walked down the porch steps and returned to his car.

CHAPTER 14

When Conrad returned to the office, he saw the list Doug Keegan had dropped off. Doug had listed the homeowners in Miriam's subdivision as well as those he knew in the Redding Realty subdivision next door. To talk to the workers, he would have to go door to door on Monday. It would be a long day.

After starting his coffeemaker, Conrad looked through the reports that Fred Rucker had left on his desk. There was a noise complaint filed by Jacob Hart against Joe Decker on two different occasions.

There was also a theft allegation made against Hart & Grace Tax Service, more specifically against Tim Grace. The reporting party had been Wyatt Tanner, a young man that worked part-time for Bryan Stotlar on the weekends as a landscaper and had his own lawn care business that he ran during the week. He had filed a report last year with Officer Tabor alleging Tim Grace stole his identity and his tax refund.

Conrad filled his coffee cup and flipped through more reports. There was another report from four years earlier where Paul Henson reported Tim Grace had altered his tax return after he had signed it. He said Tim had added additional forms to claim rebates and credits that were false which inflated Paul's refund, then Tim kept the extra money.

How did he stay in business after these kinds of allegations? And why would Jacob continue to work with him unless he was involved?

Conrad dialed the telephone number listed on Wyatt Tanner's police report and hoped it was still good.

"Hello."

"Wyatt? Wyatt Tanner?"

"Yep, that's me." Wyatt was a wiry young man who had a cheerful demeanor on the occasions that Conrad had talked with him. He had a young wife and was always eager to work. Conrad had gone fishing with him and his grandfather many times when he had first moved to town and George "Bing" Bingham, Cora Mae's husband, had been showing him around. Wyatt had been raised by his grandparents and they lived out on Eagle Bay Road near the lake.

"Hi, Wyatt. It's Chief Harris. I hope I'm not catching you at a bad time."

"No, not a bit, Chief. What can I do for you?"

"I was just looking over this old report you filed last year. You had some trouble with your income tax?"

"Oh, yeah. Tim Grace is a crook. I reported him to the IRS, too, like Eugene Tabor told me to."

"You did? What did they tell you?"

"They showed me how to file an amended return and said they'd take care of it. I guess Grace had to pay the money back. I don't know."

"Hmm, how did you find out about this?"

"Cindy and I were over in Paxton trying to buy a trailer and the financing guy had to order a copy of my last tax return because I couldn't find my copy at first. You know how they do all that credit check stuff. Anyway, once we got back home, I found it, so I took it with me when we went back over there. The guy looked at it and told me it wasn't right. He'd already gotten the copy and it didn't look like that."

"Ah," Conrad said.

"I got a copy from him and I went right over to Hart & Grace the next day. He denied everything, even with me waving the copy in his face. He's a crook!"

"Did you deal just with Tim Grace? Or did you see Jacob Hart, too?"

"Just Grace. He did up the taxes and I went by and signed them. That's when he gave me a copy."

"When you saw the real filing, did it have your signature on it?" Conrad scratched his chin.

"No, it was typed up and just had my name at the bottom. The IRS told me it was filed online."

"Oh, so it's possible he just typed in the wrong information? Maybe he put someone else's information into your return?"

"No! Can't be," Wyatt insisted. "All the business names and deductions were all the same. He just jacked up the amounts and added crazy stuff like advertising and home office expenses. There was a bunch of extra pages to it. It all looked like mine, but I don't have any fancy stuff like that. I mow yards and I pick up odd jobs here and there. I ain't never had an office and I don't do no advertising."

"So, if these changes increased your refund, why didn't the refund come straight to you? Doesn't the IRS send you a check or deposit it into your bank account?"

"Nah, Tim just paid me the day I filed. He took his fees out of my refund total and gave me the money. I guess the IRS pays him back."

"An advance refund," Conrad said.

"Yeah, that's it."

"And you've never heard anything more from the IRS?"

"No, but they said it was all square now. I tell everybody I know not to go anywhere near Hart & Grace. That's all I know to do now."

"It sounds like you did just the right thing, Wyatt. Thanks for the information."

"Sure thing. Anytime, Chief."

Conrad needed to visit the Landrys and talk to Cora Mae, but Briscoe needed a walk first. Walking down to dispatch, Conrad heard Officer Fred Rucker talking on the phone. "Yeah, he's here. Please hold."

Conrad reached for Briscoe's leash on the hook beside the dispatch entrance.

"Chief, Joe Decker is on the phone for you."

"Hmm," Conrad smiled. "Interesting. Forward the call to that desk." Conrad pointed to an officer's empty desk nearby.

"Hello Mr. Decker. How can I help you?"

"Told ya wrong."

"Excuse me? I don't understand." Conrad frowned.

"When you was here. I told ya wrong. I seen Jacob on Wednesday. Don't know if that matters."

"It could. I appreciate your help. Did you by chance see him outside earlier in the week talking with someone in the drive? A neighbor mentioned Mr. Hart had a visitor that he spoke to outside earlier in the week, but they couldn't tell who it was."

"That boy he works with. Grace, I think. He came by one night. They don't get along too well. Made a commotion, but I don't know what about."

"Do you know Jacob's son, Jeremiah?"

"He don't come around no more."

"Do you know why that is?" Conrad wrote a note to himself on a telephone message slip so he wouldn't forget to update his interview notes.

"Ask that housekeeper of his. She knows why."

"Jacob's housekeeper? Annie?"

"Yeah, she knows."

"Thank—" Conrad heard the phone click and hung up the receiver. Maybe the curmudgeon did have a conscience.

§

"Come on in," Cora said as she held open her front door for Conrad. "Dinner is not quite ready yet, but you can come in the kitchen and have a seat." Cora shuffled across the kitchen in her house slippers as Conrad slipped his coat over the back of a kitchen chair before sitting down.

"Smells good in here. Did you go to church this morning?"

"Yes, and I picked up Violet on my way. She called me yesterday when she heard about Jacob and I told her I'd swing by and get her this morning. I wanted to hear what she knew about him. Violet is a tremendous resource on the history of Spicetown citizens. Of course, she knew Jacob and his wife. I knew she would."

"Old Violet gets around?" Conrad chuckled. "Does she go to the beauty shop, too?"

"She wasn't always eighty-three, you know. She used to be very involved in all the town events and meetings. She attended everything when Bing was mayor. Between her church activities, her years as a schoolteacher, and her volunteer work, there really isn't anybody living in Spicetown that she doesn't know something about."

"So, what did you learn?" Conrad pushed his chair back so he could stroke Marmalade's back when she rubbed up against his calf.

"Jacob and Margie Hart had three children. All boys." Cora peeked in the oven at her biscuits and let the door snap shut. "Not done yet."

"What? Three? Where are the other two?"

"They drowned," Cora Mae said with her hand on her hip. "They were older than Jeremiah and when they were kids, they took a boat out on the lake, leaving Jeremiah behind. They weren't supposed to go out alone, but they did, and they told Jeremiah he better not tell on them. This was almost forty years ago."

"That's horrible."

"Jeremiah did what he was told. He didn't tell. He went back to where his parents were and he didn't say a word, even when everyone began looking for the boys."

"Ah," Conrad said nodding. "It came down on him later, huh? Did his parents blame him?"

"Violet said Jacob was never the same and he always had a rocky relationship with the boy. She felt like it stemmed back to that day."

"He was just a boy. He didn't want to get in trouble with his brothers. He couldn't have ever imagined anything like that would happen. I'm sure he just didn't want them to get into trouble with their parents."

"I agree. That's a rational explanation but it was a matter of the heart for those parents. Violet said Margie clung to Jeremiah tighter, but Jacob seemed to push him away. Maybe it was just a tragic reminder of what he lost. Some losses you never get over."

Grief marked Cora's face as memories flashed through her mind and she turned back to her stove. She was still working on managing the loss of her husband, Bing, and it had been almost fourteen years since he had passed.

After a few moments of silence, Conrad shifted in his chair. "So, they've always had a rift between them, I guess. Probably it's been difficult for them to maintain any relationship since Jacob's wife died. She probably glued the family together."

"Yes, but Violet said Jacob had other problems, too. He got into business with Tim Grace and she says that turned out to be a bad idea."

"I've heard that, too." Conrad nodded.

"I was shocked. I always thought they were close and worked well together. I had no idea there were problems."

"I had Fred pull some old reports from our files and there have been some allegations that Tim has done some unscrupulous things in the past. Nothing on Jacob, but I'd guess the risks that Tim has taken didn't set well with Jacob. That kind of thing is bad for business and hurts his integrity. I'm surprised Jacob didn't cut Tim loose and split off on his own."

"Dorothy Parish told me that her husband, Frank, and his brother, Ted, won't have anything to do with Tim Grace. She didn't know why, but I told her to ask for me. Apparently, Ted used Jacob for his business records at Chervil Drugs but there was something bad that happened in the past with Tim Grace. I just don't know the details."

"There was one report from last year. Wyatt Turner filed it. You know the young man that works part time for Bryan Stotlar?"

Cora nodded.

"Tim changed his tax return after Wyatt signed it and kept the refund money that he got for it. You can't do things like that in a small town and expect it not to ruin your business. Wyatt said he reported him to the IRS. Much more of that and Tim is going to have the feds after him. They could have closed down the business and Jacob would have lost everything. I can't believe Jacob wasn't distancing himself from Tim when he found out."

"Maybe Tim kept it from him. They were keeping their clients separate and unless Wyatt came into Hart & Grace to cause a scene when Jacob was there, it's possible Jacob didn't know." Cora Mae reached up into the cabinet for plates.

Conrad walked over to the counter and poured himself some coffee. "Is this decaf?"

"Yes," Cora said smiling.

"Do you want tea?" Conrad reached into the cabinet for a glass.

"Yes, it's over there on the counter. I just made some." Cora pointed to a glass pitcher. "Did you interview Miriam Landry yet?"

Conrad groaned. "Yes, I went over there this afternoon."

Cora Mae chuckled. "And how did that go?"

"I think they might be lying to me."

"Really!" Cora straightened her shoulders. "They were the ones looking for Jacob to start with. Why would they not be honest about when they saw him last?"

"I guess Doug Keegan could be wrong about the day, but he said Gerald was out at Jacob's house after dark Thursday night. He saw his car. He doesn't know if Miriam was with him, but he seemed pretty certain Gerald was there."

"And you asked them, and they denied it?" Cora placed a platter of fried chicken in the middle of the table and returned to the stove for the side dishes.

"Miriam denied it. She hardly let Gerald get a word in. She said they've never been out to Jacob's house after dark. They make one trip a day around mid-morning and only return in the afternoon if there is a problem. She was quite emphatic about it."

"She's emphatic about everything." Cora rolled her eyes. "Such a drama queen."

"Gerald didn't say too much. I'd like to talk to him alone and see if he says anything different."

"Now that the weather is warming, Gerald will probably start golfing again. That's his one solitary joy. Miriam hates it and it gives him an escape." Cora passed a bowl of green beans to Conrad. "He may not even like golfing. He may just do it because he knows she hates it."

Conrad laughed. "I can't think of any reason why they wouldn't want to help find out who killed Jacob. They seem to sincerely consider him a friend, and we both know Miriam doesn't have many of those."

Sheri Richey

CHAPTER 15

"Tabor, I need you to work Cumin Court for me and I'll go down Lavender Lane." Conrad hooked the leash to Briscoe's harness.

"Okay, Chief."

"We want to know if anyone saw Jacob out there last week, especially Wednesday or Thursday evening."

"The workers probably take off around four o'clock every day because they start pretty early, but the contractors might be there later. Do we have a time of death?"

"Not yet, but I expect the coroner to call this morning. If the owners aren't around, see if the contractors will give you names and phone numbers for the owners. They might be more likely to go out in the evening to look around." Conrad shook the leash and turned to walk towards the side door. "Oh, and Tabor?"

"Yeah, Chief?"

"Ask if they saw anything out there, okay? Not just Jacob, but anybody out moving around after dark around Lavender Lane. That could give us some leads on who to talk to and maybe someone saw a truck near the tree line."

"Gotcha."

"Okay, Briscoe. Let's go."

§

"Amanda, I think I'm going to walk downtown for lunch today. It's such a beautiful day."

"It always helps to have sunshine on Mondays." Amanda smiled. "Your report is due today for the City Council. I should have it on your desk when you get back so you can take a look at it before I send it out."

"Okay," Cora said as she slipped on her jacket. "I have a library board meeting this afternoon, too."

"Yes, at two o'clock."

Cora stomped her foot. "Gerald Landry should be there. He's on the library board." Cora's jaw clenched. "I can talk to him there without Miriam around."

"I didn't know you were looking for Mr. Landry."

"I'm not, but the Chief is, and he mentioned that he could never get him alone. I imagine he's too busy today to come to the library board meeting, but maybe I can help. Maybe I can talk to him while I'm there. The Chief said a witness put Gerald out at Jacob's house Thursday night, but when he asked the two of them, Miriam denied it. He hasn't had a chance to talk to Gerald alone. Perhaps Gerald was there and doesn't want Miriam to know. Or maybe Miriam is just lying."

"But why would she lie about it?"

"Hmm," Cora said. "I don't know. I always think the worst of her. You're right. It's probably nothing."

"I've been looking on the internet for some examples of merchant associations for Dorothy Parish. I wanted to email her some links so she can check out what other groups have done. She talked to Bryan about it Saturday and I think it's a really good idea. The business owners need to work together."

"Yes, she told me about her idea and I agree. It sounds like just what Spicetown businesses need. The Chamber has never supported them. Dot's a hard worker and if there's any good that can come out of it, she'll do it."

"Have you decided what you're going to do about your taxes. The time is running out. I worked on Bryan's with him all weekend and I think we're done. I just want to look it over one more time before we send it. It wasn't as bad as I thought. He kept really good records."

"That's good to hear. I may call you to help me with mine!" Cora laughed. "I guess I'll try it. I just keep putting it off. It sounds grueling to me. I don't want to spend my evening that way."

"You could get an extension," Amanda said. "I think a lot of people do that."

"Yes, but I don't know how to do that either. I might as well just quit procrastinating."

"Are you going to say anything to Ms. Fields about the Easter bunny?"

"You bet I am. I've not forgotten Saucy either. I think he's hiding from me. I plan to give them both a talking to."

Amanda laughed as Cora Mae walked out the door.

§

"Hey there, Chief." Bryan Stotlar turned off the water hose and waved. "How are you today?"

"Hey, Bryan. I'm good. I was just over at the subdivision with Briscoe. He likes to run around out there."

"Hi, Briscoe." Bryan held out his hand for Briscoe to sniff before patting him on the head. "What can I do for you?"

"Well, we're just asking around about last week. There was some trouble over in the subdivision and I didn't know if you could see much from your house. Do you remember any commotion going on over there last week after dark?"

Bryan scratched his chin. "Last week? Not that I can think of. There's always cars and trucks in or out over there, but not much traffic after dark. Sometimes I run over there and drop off materials for the next day. I'm working on the Carter's yard over in the Redding subdivision and I've done some trees at Tim Grace's house. He's not quite ready for sod yet. I like to wait until all the workers clear out and then sometimes, I take my things over there. I don't remember anything special last — Wait."

"What?"

"Well, there was someone shooting over there. At least it sounded like it came from over there." Bryan shrugged. "Out here you can hear gunshots once in a while anyway, but I was surprised when it seemed to come from the subdivisions."

"When was that?"

"One evening shortly after the sun went down, middle of the week. I'd say Thursday, but it could have been Wednesday night."

"Did you see any vehicles?" Conrad pulled his notebook from his shirt pocket.

"No, I was outside here, moving some things into the greenhouse."

"How many shots?" Conrad looked over his reading glasses at Bryan, who was frowning.

"Two, I think. That's all I remember. I looked around and didn't see anyone, but they sounded really close."

"Do the owners come out here at night much? Have you noticed any of them when you've dropped off supplies?"

"There are some that visit after the workers go home. Probably coming out when they get off work. I see Tim Grace more often than anyone. He sometimes comes during the day, too."

"Have you seen Jacob Hart?"

"Once or twice," Bryan said. "He was with the Landrys when I saw him."

"Can you see down Lavender Lane from here?" Conrad turned around and shielded his eyes with his hand. "You can see the back of the model house at Cumin Court." Conrad pointed. "I see the Millers' house and the front yard of the Lester's house, but you can't see Tim Grace's."

"No, the road doesn't line up straight so I can't see down the street. If somebody builds on the lots on Raspberry Road, I'll be able to see the north side of that street pretty clearly."

"It's probably for the best," Conrad said as he slipped his notebook back in his pocket. "If you lined up straight across, you might end up having a stoplight in your yard one day."

Bryan laughed. "My parents would be shocked if they could see all this. I can't believe my house might end up in the middle of town, eventually. When they bought this house, I was just fourteen and I thought we had moved to the boonies. Now look at it. Spicetown is really growing."

"Yeah, and with the good, sometimes comes the bad. It looks like Jacob Hart was killed over there behind his house, so you think on this for a while

and let me know if you remember anything else."
Conrad removed his reading glasses.

"Wow. Okay, Chief. I sure will."

§

"Harvey Salzman," Cora Mae called out when
she saw Saucy come out of the Spicetown Blooms
& Gift Shop across the street.

Saucy looked over and his eyes widened. "Hi,
Mayor." He stood frozen on the sidewalk and gave
a timid wave.

Cora wanted to scold him as she had her fifth
graders and tell him to get over here right now but
thought twice. She didn't want him running away
again. "Do you have a minute?" Cora motioned
him over with an innocent wave of her hand.

Saucy stepped between the parked cars and
looked both ways before crossing. "Sure, Mayor.
It's a lovely day, isn't it? How are you today?"

When he stopped in front on her, Cora reached
out and took his elbow. "I was just going into the
Caraway Café for lunch. Have you had lunch yet?"

"Oh, well no, but I—"

"Why don't you join me? I'd love to have some
company. My treat."

"Uh, well okay, ma'am. I'd be delighted."

Saucy relaxed with Cora's easy demeanor and
held the door open for her. Waving at Dorothy,
they took her favorite seat by the front window.

"Be with you in a minute," Dorothy said as she brushed by the table and Cora nodded.

"Now, Saucy, tell me about your adventure Saturday. I'm eager to hear how it went. Not the part about Jacob, but the egg hunt. Did you enjoy yourself? Do you think it is something you want to start doing every year?"

'Well, —"

"I know since Marvin has moved away, the town doesn't have an Easter bunny they can count on each year, but if you enjoyed it, it might be a good thing for you."

"I'll just have to see what next year brings." Saucy said with a shrug.

"That's true," Cora said. "You think you know how things are and how things go around here, and then something jumps up and surprises you. It's just like you, for instance. I wouldn't have ever thought you would intentionally keep something from me." Cora placed both hands over her heart. "We've been friends for so many years. I was shocked to learn that the Easter bunny that was avoiding me all morning turned out to be you! Can you imagine my shock?"

"I'm real sorry—"

"And Cece. I've known her since she was a little girl at Peppermint Elementary. I watched her grow up. She was such a pretty little thing and always did love books, even when she was that young. I would never have thought she would deceive me either. I was so surprised. The whole weekend was one shock after another and then there was Jacob. Dear Jacob, who I had been looking for all week. It's been a very unsettling time for me, Saucy. I have to tell you."

"Oh, Mayor. I'm so sorry. It wasn't like that. I mean, we never were trying to deceive you. It was just all put on for the kids and Ms. Fields didn't want to spoil anything. I was trying to do things the way she asked, and I never meant to hurt you."

"Hey, kids," Dorothy said as she appeared at the edge of the table. "What can I get you today? The special is baked ham and Frank's cheesy fried potatoes."

"Hi, Dot. I'll take the special," Cora said. "I was going to get a salad, but that sounds so much better."

"And what about you Mr. Easter Bunny? I bet you probably want a salad. Some greens, maybe?" Dorothy chuckled and propped her hand on her hip.

Saucy's eyes widened when he looked up at Dorothy and then glanced at Cora Mae. "No thank you. I've got to be going. I apologize, Mayor, but I didn't realize the time. I need to get home before one o'clock." Saucy scrambled to pull his legs out from under the table and turn in his chair.

"Uh, well. Okay, Saucy. I guess if you have to go." Cora stammered and lifted her hand to wave as Saucy backed out of the restaurant. "Have a nice day."

"You, too." Saucy turned and pushed through the front door.

"Heavens to Betsy, Cora Mae! What did you do to that little man?"

"I told him I wasn't too happy about the secrets he was keeping. I tried really hard to be nice about it, but it irked me. I guess he could tell."

"He looked scared as a rabbit." Dorothy tossed her head back and laughed.

"I should apologize to him," Cora said as she turned over the cup on the table.

"What? You should NOT do that! You didn't do anything wrong. He may have his little bunny tail between his legs for a few days, but he'll get over it. I bet he doesn't do anything sneaky again."

"I've got a library meeting today, so I'm going to talk to Cece about it. Apparently, Saucy was just doing what she told him to do."

"Doesn't she work for you? Goodness gracious! You've got to whip these people into line, Cora Mae."

Cora Mae laughed. "I might just hire you to be my muscle, Dot."

"I'm on it, girl." Dorothy pointed at Cora. "You want hot tea?"

"Yes, please."

"Coming right up." Dorothy pushed through the kitchen doors and returned through them on the second swing.

"Here you go." Dorothy slid a tiny pitcher of water on the table with a basket of tea bags. "You know, I just had a thought. Do you think Cece would let Saucy use that bunny suit again?"

"I don't know. I suppose it just sits in storage all year. What do you want with a bunny suit?"

"Frank and I talked about opening the restaurant up on Easter Sunday this year. Usually, we're closed, but since the kids aren't home and there are so many people nowadays that don't like to cook, we thought about opening for just Sunday dinner, maybe eleven o'clock to two."

"Sounds like a good idea."

"Well, if Saucy wanted to play the Easter bunny a while longer, I'd like him to pass out some flyers downtown and maybe be here Sunday. Having the Easter bunny at the café for the day would be a nice touch. Don't you think?"

Cora Mae smiled. "It sounds like a lot of fun. I'll ask Cece for you today when I see her. If she is okay loaning out the suit, you can ask Saucy about it."

"Great. I haven't taken the ad to the newspaper yet. I'll wait until I hear from you. If he can do that, I want to change my advertisement to include it."

"I'll call you as soon as I get back from the meeting."

"So, what's up with the investigation? Any ideas about Jacob?" Dorothy slid into Saucy's vacated chair across from Cora.

"Not really. I was talking to Violet yesterday and she was telling me that Jacob had two other children. Did you know that?"

"Yeah, they died really young. Jacob told me about them. The oldest was my age, so I don't remember it happening."

"It's such a shame he didn't have a better relationship with his remaining son." Cora stirred sugar into her tea.

"Maybe Jeremiah will appreciate his dad now that he's lost him. I know Jacob invited him to visit many times, but he always said he was too busy."

"It doesn't look like it." Cora shook her head. "He told Conrad he's not coming home. He'll deal with the arrangements over the phone."

Dorothy gasped. "How cold! If my kids did that, I'd jerk a knot in their tail. Even if I had to do it from the grave."

Cora smiled and rolled her eyes at the vision that created. "I bet you would."

"You know it." Dorothy leaned back in her chair. "Did Conrad figure out how Jacob ended up in the park?"

"I don't think he has all those details, but it looks like Jacob was shot at his new house, the lot out in Miriam's subdivision. I don't think he has a suspect though."

"I wish he'd never bought that lot out there. Miriam and Gerald have been all over him since he started that. He asked them to help, or maybe they offered help, but they have bugged him constantly. I think he was regretting the whole thing, too."

"Really? Did he tell you that?"

"No, but when I'd tell him Miriam had been in the café looking for him, I could see his jaw clench. They came in here several times and ruined his lunch by sitting down and starting in on him about one thing or another. He just looked miserable.

"I think he wanted a new house, but he just wanted it to happen. I don't think he wanted to deal with all the messy little details. Miriam is all about the details and she seemed to enjoy discussing every piece of trim and light socket in the place. Jacob just told her to do what she thought was best."

"He was too busy for all the tedious tasks, I'm sure." Cora Mae shook out her napkin.

"He told me he set a price for everything and he just wanted it to stay under budget. I don't think he cared about anything else."

"Oh, Amanda told me she was doing some research for you on the merchant's association. She'll probably send you an email later today or tomorrow. Have you made any decisions about that yet?"

"No, other than I'd like to do it. I just don't know if we'd have enough people involved to make it worth it. We're going to hold a meeting later this month and see who shows up."

"Be prepared for Miriam's wrath," Cora said sternly. "She may show up at your first meeting. She won't take it lying down."

"I'm looking forward to it," Dorothy said with a snarling grin. "But I don't think she's that brave."

CHAPTER 16

Officer Eugene Tabor dropped into the chair across from Conrad's desk with his notebook in his hand and crossed his ankles.

"Let's compare notes." Conrad moved his stack of paperwork to the side and slapped a legal pad on his desk. "Bryan Stotlar told me he thought he heard two gunshots Wednesday or Thursday night right after nightfall. Did you talk to anyone who can corroborate that?"

"Nope. I couldn't find anyone that was out there after dark." Eugene shook his head. "They were all workers."

"Anybody report anything unusual happening on Lavender Lane?" Conrad tapped his pen on the pad.

"Chester Callahan said that he saw Jacob Hart over at his house Wednesday night. He was in the backyard of the house and waved over at Chester when he hollered at him."

"What time was that?" Conrad slipped on his reading glasses.

"It was still light outside. He thought it was around six o'clock."

"What house is Chester working on?" Conrad scratched a note on his paper.

"Chester is working at the house on Cumin Court that is directly behind the empty lot between Jacob Hart's lot and Tim Grace's house. He said he sees Tim Grace all the time, but he doesn't really know him. He just knows who he is. Chester has known Jacob a long time."

"And did Chester see Tim Grace the night he saw Jacob?"

"Nah, he said it was just Jacob. Nothing unusual. The sun was going down, but it was still light out. As he was leaving, he said he thought the Landrys pulled up in front of Jacob's house. He didn't see them get out, but he saw her white Cadillac pull over to the curb in front of Jacob's house. He said she's there a lot."

"Hmm, yeah. I've got to talk with Gerald again about that." Conrad scowled.

"Bert Miller told me that Tim Grace was there when he left Wednesday night. He didn't notice Jacob being out there, but he said he's sure Tim Grace's truck was parked out front when he backed out to leave around six o'clock on Wednesday."

"He might not notice Jacob's car since it's four lots down." Conrad shrugged.

"That's true," Eugene said. "And Chester might not notice Tim Grace being there if he was inside his house or if Tim's truck was parked back a little."

"Yeah. It's a lot of maybes. I've got to pin Tim Grace down a little more, too."

"Sorry about that, Chief."

"Can you call the owners on Cumin Court and see if anybody was out there in the evening last week? I've got to call the coroner back. She called while we were out."

"Sure, Chief, and I'll get this written up." Officer Tabor turned to leave when Conrad nodded.

"Thanks." Conrad pulled out the phone message and glanced at the number as he reached for the phone.

"Coroner's office. Can I help you?"

"Good afternoon. This is Chief Harris in Spicetown. I've got a message to call Deputy Coroner York. Is he in?"

"Sure, Chief. Let me transfer you." Conrad flipped his page of notes over to write on the back.

"Chief! Thanks for calling back. I caught your case on Jacob Hart this weekend. Alice was off and I was on call."

"Hey, Alan. Great. So, what do you think? I could really use a time of death here."

"He was in full rigor so the best I can do is estimate his death at least six hours prior, but no more than sixty."

"Ugh," Conrad groaned. "I was really hoping for something a little more specific."

"I know, Chief. Sorry, but there's not much to go on. He died of a low velocity gunshot wound to the abdomen. It lodged in his liver and he bled to death. There was no exit wound, so I've got the bullet for comparison if you find the handgun. It's a nine-millimeter."

"No exit wound? So, it was a distance shot?" Conrad wrote the details on his notepad.

"I'd say so. No fractures were found, but we've bagged the clothes for you to send to the lab."

"There was a lot of blood at the crime scene we found, but nothing where the body was dumped. How long would it take him to bleed out?"

"I don't think very long based on the wound. If he'd been taken to a hospital right away, he might have lived. I can't give you anything exact, but I think less than an hour."

Conrad struck his notepad with the end of his pen. "I'll send somebody over there to pick up the evidence, Alan. Thanks for your help."

"Sure thing, Chief. Talk to you later."

Conrad hung up the phone slowly and rubbed his hand across his forehead. A distance shot could mean it was an accident, someone shooting recklessly into the tree line, even kids fooling around. Moving the body though, that was an act of misdirection or irrational panic and that took strength and planning.

"Hey, Chief." Officer Eugene Tabor leaned against Conrad's office door. "I just talked to Carol Sampson. She and her husband are building a house next to the model home on Cumin Court."

"Yeah?"

"She said they were both out there Wednesday evening and heard gunshots. She got a little freaked out about it and tried to get her husband to call us, but he said it was probably just somebody shooting at some varmint in their yard."

"How many shots?"

"She said it was two shots but not right together. There was one shot and after a minute or so there was another. She remembers because she started to call us after the first one and then her husband stopped her. They had a few words about it and then she heard the second one. She doesn't want to live out there if people are going to be shooting at things. I think her husband may be living in that new house all alone." Officer Tabor laughed.

"So, their house would be directly behind the Lesters' house. They probably couldn't see much since the tree line is thicker down there." Conrad tapped his pen. "Hmm, she didn't see any cars or people anywhere?"

"Nope. She just heard the shots and they left right away after that. She was frightened to be out there."

"Okay. Thanks, Tabor."

"Sure thing, Chief."

§

Cora Mae walked up the interior steps to the entrance of the main library and saw a smiling face. Elsie Flynn wiggled her fingers in a silent greeting and shuffled around the circulation desk to give Cora a hug.

"Hello, Elsie," Cora said with a soft whisper. "How are you?" Elsie Flynn had been the school librarian when Cora Mae taught fifth grade at Peppermint Elementary. When Elsie retired, she began volunteering at the Spicetown Library until they worked her right into a part-time position.

"Oh, I'm just great, Cora. You look good! That's such a pretty suit."

"Thank you."

"You're a little early for the board meeting. Would you like a cup of tea?"

"Actually, I came early because I'd hoped to chat with Cece for a few minutes. Is she around?"

"She's downstairs in the children's department."

"Will she be very long?" Cora slipped her coat off and folded it over her arm.

"Well, might be." Elsie snickered. "She's got a little situation down there."

Elsie's mischievous wink couldn't be ignored. "What's going on down there?"

Cora leaned closer and Elsie whispered in her ear. "Bridget Cunningham's little boy brought his hamster to the library in his pocket and now he can't find it."

"Oh, my. Whew," Cora said with a hiss. Shaking her head in earnest regret, she couldn't stop the small chuckle that demanded release. "Maybe I should go help her."

"Okay, but you didn't hear that from me. You know Cece. She wouldn't want anyone to know."

"I'm familiar," Cora said with raised eyebrows. "She likes her secrets."

"Secrets are things we give to others to keep for us." Elsie raised her eyebrows and gave a stern nod. "Elbert Hubbard."

Cora smiled and patted Elsie's arm. Another quote, another author she didn't know. Elsie was full of quips and quotes. "That's actually one of the reasons I wanted to talk to Cece, about one of her secrets."

"Ah, then you know about what happened to the rabbit suit Saturday."

"Hmm? No, what happened to the rabbit suit?" Cora frowned.

Elsie's eyes darted back to the circulation desk where a young man stood with a stack of books. "Oh, I've got to go, Cora. Talk later, okay?"

Cora nodded as Elsie hurried back to the counter. Leaving her coat and bag in the meeting room, Cora took the elevator down to the lower floor to look for Cece Fields in the children's department.

Cora Mae smiled as the elevator doors parted. "Good afternoon, Cece. How are you?"

Cece Fields shoved her hands back through her hair and joined her hands as she sighed. "Hello, Mayor. Is it meeting time already?"

"Not quite. I'm a bit early," Cora said as she looked around the room. There were only a few parents browsing the bookshelves with their children and the floor was quiet. "Did you have a children's reading this afternoon?"

"No. No, I just ran down here for a minute to check on a few things. I was headed upstairs to get ready for the meeting. How are things at City Hall?"

"Oh, just wonderful." Cora strolled across the opening to the aisles of audio books and beginning readers. "Your Easter display wall is lovely. Is that where you had the pictures with the Easter bunny Saturday?"

"Yes. We do the readings over by those tables, so we had to rearrange things a little."

"A good turnout?" Cora turned to Cece and raised an eyebrow.

"Oh, yes. Everyone had a great time. We had cupcakes with jellybeans on them, a reading of *It's Not Easy Being a Bunny* and then the photos with our own Easter bunny. The kids loved it!"

"That's great." Cora turned around and glared at Cece. "I guess it really wasn't easy being an Easter bunny this Saturday, was it?"

"No." Cece looked down at the floor. "I guess not."

Cora walked back to the elevator. "I guess I'll go back up. I don't want to delay you."

"I'll be up there in just a few minutes."

"Uh huh," Cora said as she turned around and stared at Cece until the elevator doors shut. They needed to have a chat once this meeting was over, a private one-on-one chat.

As the elevator doors opened, Cora Mae saw Gerald Landry at the front circulation desk chatting with Elsie.

"Afternoon, Gerald."

"Mayor! Good to see you. I was just trying to trick Elsie into waving my late fees." Gerald laughed as Elsie's cheeks pinked.

"If I were you, Elsie," Cora said with raised eyebrows. "I'd charge him double."

Elsie giggled and waved her hand dismissively at both of them. "You're going to get me in trouble, the two of you."

Gerald chuckled as he turned to head toward the meeting room.

"I saw Cece downstairs. She'll be up here in a minute. Have you seen Joyce? She may already be in the room. She's always early." Cora walked into the conference room and smiled at Joyce Miller, who was seated properly at the round meeting table. Joyce had been the Spicetown Library manager for many years and had joined the board when she retired.

"Good afternoon, Joyce. You look ready for spring!" Cora Mae pulled out a chair and put her handbag on the table. "I'm so glad we are finally seeing some sunshine."

Joyce had on a bright yellow sweater with a light pink jacket. Glancing at her watch, she tapped a pencil on her notepad. "Me, too. I'm so tired of rain. Bert and I have been working on our house and this dreadful weather keeps getting in the way."

"Oh, the new house?" Cora Mae glanced quickly at Gerald as he pulled out the chair beside her. "You are building out on Lavender Lane, aren't you?"

"Yes, but we're trying to fix up our old house on Tarragon Street because we're putting it up for sale. Bert is painting the rooms now since he can't work outside much, while I'm packing up some of our things. It's exhausting."

"I'm sure it is. Moving is always such hard work. I've lived in the same house for so long, I don't think I could move now." Cora grimaced. "I'm sure your contractor hasn't been too pleased with the rain either. Has it delayed the workers much?"

"I don't think so. They're working inside most of the time now. Horrible thing that happened to Jacob," Joyce said looking at Gerald. "I was so sorry to hear about that."

Gerald nodded. "Shocking."

"Yes, it was," Cora said as other members began to join them and Cece walked in to greet everyone. "Gerald," Cora Mae said in a low voice. "When the meeting is over, do you have a few minutes?"

"Sure, Mayor." Gerald nodded.

"The Chief would like to talk to you. Do you think you could run over to the station when we're done here? I know he doesn't want to bother you at home."

"I'll do that. No problem." Gerald gave another curt nod and then turned his attention to Cece as the meeting began.

Sheri Richey

CHAPTER 17

"Chief!" Officer Fred Rucker grasped the wood trim around Conrad's office door and leaned into the doorway. "Asher's on the phone. He needs to talk to you."

Fred didn't often get up and leave the dispatch cubicle or become flustered easily, but his words were rushed. Rather than running back to dispatch, Fred pointed at Conrad's desk phone and waited.

"Asher?" Conrad barked into the receiver. "What's going on?"

"I found Jacob Hart's car. I can't get inside. It's locked, but it looks like there's blood in the back. What do you want me to do?"

"Don't touch it!" Conrad barked. "Where are you?"

"At the Wasabi, Chief. They aren't open yet and I just noticed there was a white SUV just sitting here alone, so I had Fred run the plates. It's Jacob's."

"Okay, well we need to print the outside of it first and then get it towed. Can you do that?" Conrad reached for his coffee cup and saw it was empty.

"Yeah, sure. Sure, Chief. You want it towed to the city garage?"

"Yes. Make sure you print all the door handles and around the back hatch or edges of the rear door where someone might have lifted it up or down."

"Gotcha," Officer Asher said and sighed heavily into the phone receiver. "Can you ask Fred to call the tow for me?"

"Yeah. Now, make sure you lock it up at the garage. Good job, Asher."

"Aw, thanks, Chief."

"What were you doing out at the Wasabi, anyway? It doesn't open for almost two hours." The Wasabi Women's Club was a dance club on the west edge of Spicetown and Officer Asher was often teased about his fondness for it.

"It's my turn around spot, Chief. When I patrol the west side, I go out to the Wasabi and turn around."

"Hmm, okay." Conrad chuckled. He suspected Asher was hoping the girls were starting to show up for work. He liked to chat them up when he had a chance. "Let me know when it's secure. Oh, and Asher, don't dawdle. Try to get it out of the parking lot quickly before anyone starts showing up for work."

"I will."

Conrad hung up the phone and looked at Fred. "Call a tow to go out there, will you? No rush. It'll probably take him half an hour to print the doors."

Fred Rucker gave Conrad a thumbs up signal and disappeared back to his station.

§

"Cece, can we talk for a minute?" Cora walked over and pulled out the chair at the board room table next to Cece's and waited patiently as everyone said their goodbyes.

Returning to her seat, Cece pushed her chair back and turned. "What can I do for you, Mayor?"

"Well, first off I was happy to hear your Easter event went well and I wondered if you had any plans for the Easter bunny suit this week. Do you have any readings planned for the children?"

"No, it was only on Saturday afternoon. I was going to contact Mr. Salzman about this coming Saturday, the Saturday before Easter Sunday, but I don't know if he's free."

"Well, Dorothy Parish from the Caraway Café approached me and asked if they could borrow the suit. They are advertising for an Easter Sunday dinner and thought it would be fun to have Saucy hand out flyers in the bunny costume. Would you mind at all?"

Cece cringed and deep lines formed across her forehead. "Ordinarily, no, but the suit isn't clean. There was a little accident on Saturday and I'm not sure how to get it cleaned. The Peppercorn Cleaners aren't sure they can get a stain out of the white fake fur, but I was going to take it down there this afternoon and have someone look at it."

"Oh, dear. I didn't realize anything had happened. It's not blood, is it?"

"Oh, no. No, it's just chocolate milk. One of the kids spilled it on Mr. Salzman when they bumped into him, but it's a large stain."

"Well, I'll run it over to the cleaners for you when I leave here. It's almost on my way and I'll see if there's anything they can do."

"Thank you," Cece said.

"On a similar note, I do want to make something clear for future events."

Cece frowned.

"In the future, I want you to share with me who you've selected for your volunteers. It was very disturbing to me to think this Easter event was kept secret. I understand that you wanted to keep the mystery alive for the kids, but I am not a child, and when the Easter egg hunt turned into a murder investigation, it was not helpful that no one knew who found the body. Now, hopefully nothing as significant as that will happen at future events, but one can never be too certain."

Cece nodded. "I'm sorry, Mayor. I didn't intentionally keep Mr. Salzman a secret from you.

I just told my staff to keep it quiet and they did a better job than I expected." Cece gave a half-hearted smile.

"I see." Cora looked down at her hands clasped in her lap. "And the hamster downstairs?" Cora looked up and raised her eyebrows. "Did you feel you needed to conceal that also?"

Cece hesitated and turned her chair to face the table. "I wasn't concealing that either, Mayor. When you arrived downstairs, the hamster had been found. There was nothing to report."

"Hmm, well, okay dear. I just want to make certain that you don't think you have to keep secrets from me. I'm not judging you. I'm here to support you, but I do want to be aware of the decisions you make, not just as a member of the library board, or the mayor. I think we need to work on our communication a little and I wanted my expectations to be clear."

"I understand, Mayor. I just wanted everything to go well." Cece's voice wavered. "I didn't want it to look like I couldn't do my job."

"Goodness, no. Having problems is something you take for granted when you do a job right, any job. Do you think my day goes smoothly? Ha! It's utter chaos sometimes." Cora Mae huffed. "Don't try to control your surroundings. Just learn to go with the flow and share those bumps and potholes with anyone who can help you. In this community we hold each other up and you need to get on board!"

Cece smiled. "I'll try to do that, Mayor."

"Good!" Cora stood and slipped on her coat. "Now bag up that bunny suit and I'll hit the road."

Cece jumped from her seat and scurried into her office, returning with the bunny head under one arm and a large shopping bag for the suit and shoe covers in the other. "Let me carry these out to your car for you."

"Tell Violet I said hello," Elsie called out as Cora followed Cece to the front door.

"I will, dear. You take care."

§

"Gerald," Conrad said with his hand extended to shake. "Thanks for coming in."

"Happy to help," Gerald Landry said, returning the handshake. "The mayor said you needed to talk with me."

"I do. I wasn't able to really get a chance to hear your side of things when I came by your house and there are some specific points I need to be clear about."

Gerald took a seat across from Conrad's desk and nodded.

"Wednesday night. Do you remember what time you went out to Jacob's new house?"

"Before nightfall," Gerald said. "I'd guess about five o'clock, maybe a little after."

"How long did you stay?"

"Until Jacob showed up. I called him and left him a message that I was there and asked if he could swing by when he got off work."

"And he did."

"Yeah. We talked for about half an hour and I left. He had some things he wanted to measure or something. I don't remember what he said specifically, but he wasn't ready to leave yet."

"Do you know what time you left?"

Gerald's forehead creased as his eyes traveled around the room. "I don't really. It was dark or just getting dark it seems like."

"Okay, so you arrived around five o'clock. When did Jacob get there?"

"Conrad, I don't really know. Whatever I tell you will just be a guess. It was just a normal day and I'm retired. I don't watch the clock much."

"Did Miriam know you were out there?"

"I told her about it later, after she got back to town. She was in Paxton all afternoon."

"And she took your car?"

"Yeah!" Gerald said in surprise. "How did you know that?"

Conrad shrugged innocently and Gerald continued.

"She had to pick up some things she ordered and needed my SUV, so I took her car to Hank's that afternoon and got her oil changed."

"Do you own a gun, Gerald?"

Gerald sat up straight in his chair. "You know I do, Conrad. Why would you—"

"Do you know where it is? Can you bring it by the station?"

"Well, yeah. I can, but what do you want with my gun? I didn't shoot Jacob."

"I didn't say you did, but I need to account for these things. How long has it been since you used it or saw it?"

"Probably six months." Gerald slumped back down in his chair.

"Okay, so when you went out to the house around five o'clock on Wednesday, did you see Tim Grace or Bert Miller out there?"

"I don't think so, but you know, I'm out there about every day. All these days run into each other. I see Bert and Tim off and on all the time. I can't be sure about it."

"My understanding is that you and Miriam visit daily, usually in the mid-mornings. Visiting in the evening without Miriam isn't customary. Isn't that correct?"

"Well, yeah. I guess, but Conrad, it wasn't a big deal. I mean, it wasn't all that memorable. Jacob's a friend. Miriam was out of town and we just had some time to knock around out there."

"Assuming Jacob arrived by six o'clock, you still had almost two hours of daylight. If you left at sundown, you chatted for two hours, not thirty minutes. Did you leave and come back?"

"Yeah, I went back to town and got us something to eat. It seems like Tim and Tonya Grace were parked out there when I came back, but I don't remember seeing Bert Miller."

Conrad leaned back in his chair. That would explain Chester's sighting of the white Cadillac arriving at dusk. "Okay, so you stayed and had a bite to eat with Jacob?"

Gerald nodded.

"Maybe you had a few beers?" Conrad raised an eyebrow. Officer Tabor had reported finding a large quantity of crushed beer cans in a trash bag on the side of the house. Hopefully, the construction workers were not drinking on the job.

"Yeah, with our dinner."

"Where did you get dinner?" Conrad leaned forward in his chair prepared to write.

"Good grief, Conrad. Do you want to know what I was wearing?" Gerald threw his hands up in the air and let his hands slap down on his thighs.

"Sure," Conrad nodded with a smirk. "Or even better, what was Jacob wearing?"

"I don't know," Gerald shouted in frustration.

"Look, Gerald. You are very possibly the last person to see Jacob Hart alive. I need to know everything you saw, everything he said, everything you can remember about what was going on out in that subdivision Wednesday night. It's important."

"Okay," Gerald said after a relaxing exhale. "I understand."

"Did Jacob mention anything to you about being stressed about anything? Anyone he was having difficulty with or arguing with? Or just anything new going on in his life?"

"Jacob had a simple life. He really didn't do much away from home or work. He worked long hours. He liked to garden and he read a lot, but he had a peaceful life."

"Did he ever talk about his neighbor, Joe Decker?"

"Yeah, the guy made a lot of noise and he made a complaint about it. Nothing recently though."

"What about Tim Grace? Did he talk about him?"

"He and Tim haven't gotten along in years. He helped set Tim up in business and taught him everything he could, but Tim never kept up his end of the deal. When he brought him into the business, Tim agreed to take night classes to get his degree so he could work into a partner or take over the business when Jacob retired, but after he put his name on the door, Tim started backing out of the agreement."

"He didn't want to be a partner?"

"Oh, yeah. He wanted to take over everything, but he wouldn't go back to school to do it the right way. He told Jacob he didn't need that. He could do the same work that Jacob did without all that wasted money on education. Tim's a cocky guy. He thinks he's smarter than everyone else."

"So, why didn't Jacob take his name off the door?"

"I don't really know. I suggested that a few times. Maybe there was something in their agreement that kept him from it. He never said. I know they kept their work separate. Tim messed some of Jacob's accounts up years ago and Jacob told him to keep his hands off his clients. Since then, they've worked independently."

"Do they argue often?"

"I don't think they really even talk anymore. Jacob hasn't mentioned him lately, but I know that's why he bought the lot down at the end. He didn't want to be next to Tim."

"So, you haven't seen Tim and Jacob talk out at the work site?"

"No, not once." Gerald said. "Jacob was talking several months ago about selling the business to a guy in Red River, but that fell through. He did some research and decided the guy wasn't reputable. I guess he still has the ownership rights. He doesn't talk like Tim is a part owner."

"Do you know if Tim and Jacob had a legal agreement of some sort?"

"Nah, I don't. He said they had an agreement, but I don't know if it was put down on paper."

"Have you heard from Jacob's son, Jeremiah? Someone has to handle Jacob's personal and business affairs. I'm assuming that responsibility lies with Jeremiah."

"I haven't heard anything from him, but I don't think he'd call me. He's cut all ties with Spicetown. Ned Carey might know something. He handled Jacob's legal matters."

"Do you know what got between Jacob and Jeremiah?"

"They were never close. There was always conflict between them but after Margie died, there was no one around to referee. Jeremiah got it in his head that Jacob was seeing Annie Radford. Jacob gave Annie something that had belonged to Margie and Jeremiah went ballistic about it. There were a lot of accusations made until finally they just parted company. I don't think they've talked at all since then."

"Okay." Conrad nodded and pushed back his chair. "Thank you, Gerald. You've been really helpful. Please let me know if you think of anything else."

Gerald nodded as he rose from his chair.

"Oh, and you can bring the gun by tomorrow anytime. Dispatch will give you a receipt for it."

CHAPTER 18

"Well, hello, Mayor! How are you?" Charles Talbot walked up to the counter of the Peppercorn Dry Cleaners when the entry doorbell chimed.

"I'm fantastic, Charlie. How are you?"

"It's a busy day, so it's a good day. What can I do for you and your furry friend?" Charlie chuckled when Cora looked down at the bunny head she carried under her arm.

"I'm dropping this off for Cece Fields. She had a little spill on Saturday, and we wanted you to take a look and see if you thought you could get it out. Cece said it was chocolate milk." Cora pulled the costume out of the shopping bag and stretched it out on the counter to find the stain. "I don't know when it was last cleaned, but we used it Saturday morning at the egg hunt and then at the library in the afternoon. I was hoping we could get it back quickly so we could use it a few more times this week before Easter is over."

"Hmm," Charles hummed as he stroked his chin and turned the fabric over to look at the inside. "I think we can get this out and clean the suit up by the end of the day tomorrow. I can't do anything for the head though. That fur is glued on."

"Getting the stain out is the first worry, so I'm happy you can do that." Cora placed the bunny head on the counter and pulled out her notepad. "I can have someone pick it up tomorrow after four o'clock. Can I pay you for it today?"

"Oh, no bother. We'll bill you. I don't want to charge you until I'm sure we can get it clean. Do you have other Easter events going on this week?"

"No, but Dorothy Parish had asked to borrow the costume to have someone hand out flyers for her. The Caraway Café is going to offer dinner on Easter Sunday this year."

"That's nice. I'll be sure and have it ready for pickup tomorrow. Have you heard anything more about Jacob Hart? There was almost nothing in the newspaper. Do they have any idea who shot him?"

"I know they're working on it. I haven't talked to the Chief today. I don't even know if he has the coroner's report yet."

"Jacob was just in here last week. You just never think that you might be seeing someone for the last time, you know." Charlie shook his head and sighed. "We've always done all of Jacob's shirts and slacks since Margie died so he comes in every week. I can't believe someone killed him."

"Did you notice anything different about him or did he talk to you about anything going on in his life?" Cora realized that Jacob talked to everyone in the community, yet no one knew anything about him. As a single man, he ate most meals out, had a housekeeper, and dropped off his laundry at the cleaners. Even sharing his office space didn't offer any opportunity for him to bond with anyone. Who was his confidante?

"No, same as always." Charlie shrugged.

"Thank you, Charlie, and I'll get it picked up tomorrow." Cora waved as she walked out the door carrying the bunny head under her arm.

§

Conrad walked out of the break room with a pitcher of water for his coffeemaker in his hand just as Officer Eugene Tabor walked in the front door. "Tabor, are you free right now?"

"Yeah, Chief. I just clocked in at four."

Conrad waved at Eugene to follow him down the hallway as he kept his eye on the water level in the pitcher. "Have a seat." Pouring the water into the back of the coffee maker and snapping the top shut, Conrad returned to his desk. "Asher found Jacob Hart's car today."

"Wow. Where was it?"

"Parked out at the Wasabi."

Eugene chuckled. "Whoever did that must not know that Asher checks that lot every hour."

"Well, I called Wendell and told him to pull all the tapes of the parking lot since Wednesday. He should have them ready for pickup by now. We may not see much on them depending on where the SUV was parked, but we'll need to watch them and see when it got there."

"You want me to go pick them up?"

"Yes, and then I want you go out to the city garage and go through the car. Asher printed the outside doors before it was towed and it's supposed to be locked up out there. We need to pop those doors and see what's inside. Asher thinks there's blood in the back."

"You think they moved his body to the park in his car?"

"Could be. We might find some trace evidence in there."

"You know, Chief. I've been out to the Wasabi a few dozen times, not as much as Asher, of course," Tabor said with a grin. "But enough to know the regulars out there."

"Was Jacob Hart a regular?"

"No, Chief. Not that I know about, but Tim Grace, he's out there a lot."

"Really?" Conrad hummed. "Do you ever see Gerald Landry out there?"

"No. Do you think he's involved in Jacob Hart's murder?" Tabor leaned forward with his elbows on his knees.

"He's the last person I know of that saw Jacob Hart alive. I know they were drinking together that night out at his new house and I know Gerald owns a handgun. That's where the beer cans came from that you found outside."

"You think maybe it was an accident? Two old guys drinking too much and — "

"I've not thought that far ahead yet. There's still a lot we don't know. We need the security tapes from the Wasabi. Wes has a camera on the parking lot."

"Okay, Chief. I'll get on it."

§

"Morning, Mayor." Amanda lifted a box of files from the floor to her desktop.

"Good morning, Mandy. Whatever are you up to now?" Cora slipped her arm from her jacket and sat her purse in a chair. "You're going to hurt yourself."

"I'm moving all the old files out and sealing them to go upstairs into storage. We need room in the cabinets."

"You can't carry all that up there."

"No," Amanda said, crouching down to the next drawer. "Rodney said he would stop back in later and take them up for me."

"Ah, that's nice. Rodney's such a nice boy." Cora Mae took a moment to visualize Rodney Maddox someday sitting in Jimmy Kole's chair as

Superintendent of Spicetown Streets & Alleys once Jimmy took her job. Succession planning was always going on in the back of her mind. "I know I have a City Council meeting this afternoon, but is there anything going on this morning?"

"No, nothing on the calendar. Violet Hoenigberg called for you this morning and I left a note on your desk, but you don't have any appointments."

"Good. I wonder what Violet needs. I'll go check on her. Don't you strain your back, now."

"I won't."

Cora dropped her purse into her bottom desk drawer and called Violet on her cell phone. "Violet? Amanda said you called this morning."

"Yes, Cora. I got to thinking after we talked at church and last night, I called Geraldine to check with her. Sometimes I have to test my memory a little, but I thought I remembered her telling me something about Annie Radford. It's been a few years, though."

"Geraldine knows Annie?"

"Yes, but it was something Melody told her. She heard it from Rhonda, who got to know Cindy Malone at the tan place when she was dating Quentin. Anyway, the rumor was that Jeremiah accused Jacob of having an affair with Annie."

"When was this?"

"Oh, fifteen years ago, I guess. Annie's husband was gone but it was before Margie died."

"What caused him to make that accusation? Annie and Margie were close friends, I thought." Cora rested her forehand in the palm of her hand.

"He found something, something with Annie's name on it. A love letter, maybe. She couldn't remember the details either, but apparently Jeremiah had a hissy fit about it, and it caused a big argument between them."

"Surely Jeremiah isn't still holding on to that anger."

"I don't know," Violet said with a huff. "He went so far as to accuse Jacob of fathering Annie's son. It was pretty heated."

"Oh, mercy. Annie must have set him straight. Quentin looks just like Sam Radford. I can't believe anyone would question his paternity."

"Geraldine said Margie is the one that calmed him down. She told him she and Jacob had both had a life before they were married, and it wasn't any of his business. I guess maybe Jacob and Annie dated when they were young."

"Or it could have been someone else named Annie," Cora said. "I agree with Margie. Either way, it was none of Jeremiah's business."

"Well, Melody said it was the last time Jeremiah was here in Spicetown until his mother's funeral."

"That's a gloomy note, to know the last time the family was together it was to argue." Cora shook her head.

"Families are complicated sometimes."

"Well, thank you, Violet. I'll let the Chief know." Cora made a short note on her desk pad.

"Okay, dear. Talk to you later."

Cora Mae pulled out her desk drawer and tossed her phone in her purse.

"Amanda, did you ever find any information on the merchant association for Dorothy Parish?"

"Yes, I sent her an email with a number of links. The ones in the cities have all kinds of benefits to offer, but it should give her some ideas. Apparently, they just call a meeting, draft a charter, and have an election. That's all there is to it, so once she figures out what she wants to offer, she's ready to go."

"From what I gathered, Dot is not very comfortable with internet searching and I know her time is limited. She may need some help from us. If Jacob were still alive, I bet he'd offer a reduced price for tax help to the members."

"Did you ever do your taxes?" Amanda stood up from her crouched position over the files and stretched her back.

"No, but it's on my To-Do list. Maybe one night this week I'll try to figure it out."

"Bryan's is all done. I won't let him put it off this long next year. I'm not sure what my folks are going to do next year. They're just like you. They've depended on Jacob for a long time."

"Maybe someone new will come along soon. Jacob had a lot of clients and from what I hear, they don't want to go to Tim Grace. I don't know what will become of the business now that Jacob's gone. I wonder if Ned Carey knows. I think I'll give him a call."

Amanda smiled as Cora grabbed for her desk phone.

Sheri Richey

CHAPTER 19

"There he is, with his mystery coffee. Morning, Connie." Ned Carey was the Spicetown City Attorney and owned the Sweet & Sour Spice Shop on Ginger Street. He had a comfortable business handling the town's needs and helping the business owners, but he had sworn off domestic law years ago.

"I'm getting rather attached to it," Conrad said as he swirled his thermal mug. "I keep forgetting to ask the mayor what it is."

Ned raised his eyebrows and chuckled. "But is it helping?"

"It is, as much as I hate to admit it," Conrad said with a smirk. "That's just between us."

Ned tossed his head back and laughed.

"You want a cinnamon roll, Chief?" Vicki wiped the table off with a wet cloth.

"Yeah. Thanks, Vicki." Conrad walked down to the Fennel Street Bakery almost every morning and had coffee with his regular gang. Today Ned was the first to arrive. "Before the other guys get here, I wanted to talk to you about Jacob Hart. I heard you handled some legal work for him, and I thought you might know something that could help me out."

"What do you need to know?" Ned leaned forward and lifted his coffee cup to take a sip.

"Do you know what his legal arrangements were? Does Tim have any legal rights to the business?"

"No, they never drew up any contracts. They talked about it and if Tim had gotten his CPA license, there might have been, but nothing more than talk."

"Then why was Tim's name on the door?" Conrad nodded his thanks to Vicki as she placed the pastry in front of him and rushed off.

"I think it was a gimmick. The names went together well, but Jacob saw Tim as a protégé at first and treated him like the son he wished he'd had. He had confidence that Tim would complete the education and follow in his footsteps. A few years in, things went south."

"So, it was good in the beginning?"

"Oh yeah, until Tim started screwing things up and Jacob lost patience with his failure to keep his end of the bargain. He never enrolled in classes and it finally came to a head when Tim told him he wasn't wasting his time with it. They've just coexisted since then.

"Tim had already developed a clientele of his own that wasn't the type Jacob wanted. He thought Tim filled a need in the community for people who wanted a quick easy tax preparation and he let Tim handle those. Jacob didn't have time for that anyway."

"Any business recently? Had Jacob come to see you about anything?"

"No, but his boy, Jeremiah, has been blowing up my phone."

"Really?" Conrad wiped his fingers on a napkin. "What does he want from you?"

"The will." Ned wiggled his eyebrows up and down. "He's not entitled to it, though. Ohio law spells out just who can have a copy and he's not the guy."

"So, Jacob didn't leave his property to his son?" Conrad sat back in his chair.

"Nope. He's got to wait a month until we go to probate. No one else has stepped up."

"So, the person named doesn't know that they've inherited a business and two houses?"

"I guess not." Ned shrugged and waved a hand in the air when Ted Parish, the owner of Chervil Drugs, walked in the front door. "Or maybe they're just shy."

Conrad smirked. "It would help me to know who it is. Did he leave everything to one person?"

"No. He left specific instructions and he didn't leave Jeremiah out, but he didn't make him executor, so he has to wait until the probate court processes the will to find out the details."

"I need to see a copy of that will, Ned."

"I know," Ned said. "Cora Mae already hit me up about that this morning. I'll scan a copy and send it over to you."

"Was Cora in here?" Conrad looked around the bakery.

"No, she called my office first thing this morning and I told her I would share it with you to help with the investigation, but it wasn't for public knowledge."

"I haven't heard from her today."

"I guess great minds just think alike." Ned laughed as Ted Parish joined the morning coffee gang carrying a banana nut muffin.

"Morning, Ted," Conrad said before taking a bite of his cinnamon roll.

"Hey, Conrad. How are things going with your case? Have you found anything out yet?"

"We're working on it, Ted. How long have you known Jacob?" Conrad brushed crumbs from his fingers and picked up his coffee mug.

"I can't remember not knowing him, so I guess it's been over fifty years. I'm not sure what I'm going to do without him. He's done my books for years. I'm not letting Tim Grace touch anything, so I've got to find someone to replace Jacob quickly. I checked on a couple of firms in Paxton, but I'm thinking that I need to just hire an accounting clerk on my staff who does all that for me and then I can get a CPA to just do my annual taxes. I never realized what a deal Jacob was giving me. These other guys want to charge twice what I was paying Jacob."

"You don't get any buddy discounts when you go to Paxton," Ned said. "That's for sure."

"Have either of you seen Jeremiah in the last couple of years? I hear he and Jacob were estranged, but I don't know how long ago that happened."

"He hasn't lived in Spicetown since he went away to college and that was almost twenty years ago." Ted stirred his coffee and took a sip. "He used to come visit some before Margie died, but I haven't seen him in years."

"You mentioned not letting Tim Grace touch your books," Conrad said. "You don't like Tim?"

Ted looked over the top of his glasses at Conrad and then over to Ned. "He doesn't know?"

Ned shrugged.

"Tim Grace is a shyster. I would have thought you'd know that." Ted pointed at Conrad.

"No, I didn't. This weekend I found two old reports that raised some questions about his tax preparation skills, but no one has ever reported anything else. What makes you say he's a shyster?"

"I guess I shouldn't say that," Ted said leaning back in his chair. "I mean I can't prove it, but he messed some of my books up when he first started, and Jacob just told me he'd keep him away from my accounts. He pushed it off as inexperience, but I don't think that's what it was. I think the boy was trying to cook my books!"

Ned Carey chuckled. "What Ted is trying to say is that he felt like Tim put down incorrect figures so he could skim money from his accounts."

"Embezzlement." Conrad leaned his elbows on the table. "Ted, when was the last time you saw Jacob?"

"Week before last. He was eating lunch at Frank's and I stopped in to pick up my order. I just waved at him. We didn't talk."

"He ate lunch at the Caraway Café almost every day through the week," Ned said. "I saw him in there once in a while too."

"Oh, the office is calling me," Conrad said as he glanced at his vibrating cell phone. "I guess I better get back to work. You two stay out of trouble."

§

"Hey there," Amanda said when she answered her cell phone. Bryan rarely called during the workday. He had Stotlar Nursery to run and even if he didn't have customers, he had a lot of work to do in his greenhouse.

"Hi, honey. Sorry to bother you at work, but do you know what's going on out here?"

"No," Amanda hesitated. "What's going on out there?"

"There are cop cars everywhere. The Chief's out here and there are other patrol cars. They are all pulled over on North Road just before you get to my house."

"Oh, my. Let me go see if the mayor knows anything about it. Hold on." Amanda jumped from her seat and hurried around her desk.

"Mayor?" Amanda tapped lightly on the door frame to Cora's office and Cora looked up from her computer. "Bryan's on the phone and he said the Chief is out on the North Road with several other squad cars. Have you heard anything? Has something bad happened out there?"

"Why, no. I haven't heard from the Chief at all today. Let me call the station and see if I can find out from Georgia."

Cora Mae reached for the phone and dialed.

"Spicetown Police Department. Officer Marks speaking. How may I help you?"

"Hello, Georgia. It's Cora Mae. I won't keep you—"

"Hey, Mayor. The Chief's not in right now."

"Yes, I know he's out on North Road and that's why I was calling. Can you tell me what the trouble is out there? Nothing new with the subdivision, I hope."

"Nah, just Jack Rabbit Robbins. His truck ran out of gas and he was walking to town and he found a gun on the side of the road. He called it in and the Chief's out there checking it out."

"Oh, my. You think it might be the murder weapon?"

"I don't know. Might be. That's why the Chief went out there to get it. Jack Rabbit didn't say what kind of condition it was in. If might have been out in the weather a long time and not even be connected to the murder."

"Okay. Well, thank you. I'll talk to the Chief later."

Cora hung up the phone and looked at Amanda. "They found a gun on the side of the road. I bet someone threw it out of their car window after they shot Jacob."

Amanda gasped. "Let me go tell Bryan to stay inside. He always thinks he needs to go out and help everybody. He's going to get himself shot one of these days."

"That's just speculation on my part. I don't know if it is related to Jacob or not."

Amanda ran off to grab the phone. Cora Mae chuckled to see the protective mother hen emerge in Amanda whenever Bryan's welfare was questioned.

§

"Sorry I'm a little late," Conrad said as he scooted over in the booth at the Old Thyme Italian Restaurant holding his plastic travel mug in the air. "Had to make some fresh coffee before I came.

I've gotten used to toting this mug around with me now."

"But has it helped? Do you feel better without coffee?"

"I don't want to talk about it," Conrad grumbled.

Cora Mae laughed. "The doc may have cured your heartburn. Next time ask him how to cure the grumpiness."

"Good evening," the waiter said. "Can I get you both something to drink?"

"I'd like some hot tea," Cora said.

"Just some water, please." Conrad looked over suspiciously at Cora and waited for the man to leave. "Who was that?"

"I think that's Sally Gilmore's nephew. Her sister just moved back to town and she has two children I've not met yet." Cora watched the young man through squinted eyes.

"What's on the back of his head?" Conrad said in a low voice as he leaned forward.

"I believe they call that a man bun, Conrad."

"A man bun! You've GOT to be kidding."

"Unfortunately, no," Cora said with a dismissive wave of her hand. "Nevertheless, what did you learn today? I hear you found a gun. Does it look like it could be the murder weapon?"

"Looks that way. At least it's not been outside long, and it holds nine millimeter shells. I'm going to send it in for testing. The coroner's office has the bullet. We printed it, but that's not likely to be any help."

"How did your talk with Gerald Landry go? He said he would go straight over there after the library meeting."

"He did. He's a little defensive. I have mixed feelings about that interview. He got a little hot with me for asking questions about the last evening he says he was with Jacob. He acts like he has something to hide and Gerald is usually pretty easy going."

"So, they did see Jacob. They told you when you first interviewed them that they didn't."

"Different day," Conrad said shrugging. "When I talked to them first, I thought this went down Thursday night, but it looks like it was Wednesday, and Gerald was with him that night. Miriam wasn't there and I think it's possible that Miriam doesn't even know about it. That may be why he's so testy. Miriam was out of town and I don't think Gerald wants her to know he was out at Jacob's new house drinking."

"Drinking?" Cora Mae hummed. "Perhaps Miriam doesn't permit that."

"Perhaps," Conrad said with a chuckle.

"Are you ready to order?"

Conrad looked up and peered around the young man's head. "Whatcha got your hair tucked up in, young man?"

Cora Mae's cheeks pinked.

"Uh, just a rubber band, sir." The young man patted the back of his head and then turned his head to show Conrad.

"Hmm, so it is," Conrad said.

"Did you see the specials when you came in? I can give you a few more minutes if you like."

Cora hated to delay the waiter's ordeal, so she ordered her usual and waited for Conrad to do the same.

"I'll put your orders right in."

Cora noticed the waiter glance back over his shoulder before he walked away, probably to see if Conrad was looking, and Conrad did not disappoint him.

"You'll make the young man self-conscious," Cora scolded.

"He ought to be, walking around with a hairdo like that. What's he thinking?"

"It's better than finding his long dark hair in your salad."

"Hmm, yeah. I guess you're right about that." Conrad huffed. "It's still ridiculous."

"Didn't you ever have long hair, Conrad? What about the sixties or the seventies?" Cora held her palms out.

"Nope. I was in the service and if I did something silly like that, they'd have shaved my whole body bald before they shaved my head."

Cora Mae laughed. "Okay. I give up. Did you find anything interesting in Jacob's car?"

"Tabor picked up a few things. Some longish light-colored hairs off the driver's seat, obviously not Jacob's. There was a lot of blood in back, so that was probably how the body was moved to the park and he found a pink fake fingernail. He'll get it all shipped to the lab tomorrow."

"Did you connect with Ned Carey today?"

"Oh yeah. He said you called him this morning. He sent me a copy of the will."

"What did it say?" Cora lifted her shoulders and sat up straight.

"He told me I couldn't tell you," Conrad smirked.

"Uh! He did NOT." Cora Mae squared her shoulders.

Conrad chuckled at Cora's indignant response. "He told me it was supposed to be secret until it went through probate."

"Well, when is that?"

"Not for a month."

"I can't wait a month, Conrad. What does it say?"

"He left his new house to Jeremiah, the one he's building. That's something he added a few months ago after he bought the lot."

"What about the business? Did he leave it to Tim?"

"No, Tim isn't mentioned. Ned says he talked about it a few years ago and if Tim had kept his end of their agreement, Jacob might have done that, but not now. It will have to be closed or sold by the executor."

"Who is the executor?"

"Ned Carey," Conrad said. "Ned says that Jeremiah can contest that when the will goes to probate, but he doesn't think he'll win any points since they've been estranged for years and Jeremiah is named to receive some property."

"Who is getting the old house? Jacob hadn't even put it on the market yet."

"Ned said he didn't plan to sell it. He always planned to give it to Annie Radford and that's who is named in the will. Even if he had lived, he was going to deed it over to her once he moved into his new house."

"Oh my," Cora said with a hand covering her mouth. "Maybe that story I heard was true."

"What story?" Conrad leaned closer.

"Well, I heard that the last time Jeremiah was in town visiting about fifteen years ago, he accused Jacob of having an affair with Annie Radford and suggesting he might be Quentin Radford's real father. Naturally, it wasn't well received and although Margie calmed him down, he left town angry. Except for Margie's funeral, he hasn't come back to visit."

"Where did this story come from? Were you at the beauty shop again?"

Cora Mae huffed. "No, Connie. The story is coming from Melody, who is Geraldine's niece. You know Geraldine, Violet's friend."

Conrad groaned. "And how does Melody know this?" After a moment's hesitation Conrad waved his hands in the air. "No, forget I asked that."

Ignoring Conrad's gesture, Cora Mae continued. "Melody's best friend, Rhonda, works at the

Safflower Sundown Tan Shop on Tarragon Street. One of their regular customers is Cindy Malone and she used to date Quentin Radford. Cindy told her about it."

Conrad groaned louder.

Cora pointed her schoolteacher index finger across the table at Conrad. "You really should talk to Annie and Quentin."

CHAPTER 20

"Morning, Tabor," Conrad said as Officer Eugene Tabor walked by his office door. "Are you all done with the car now?"

"Yeah, Chief. I'll get it all sent to the lab today. There wasn't much in the car, but I bagged all the contents. I'll get you an inventory list."

"Well, if you can get all that done in a couple of hours, I'd like to take you with me for an interview. I don't want to go too early, but I need to go see the Radfords."

"Quentin Radford?" Tabor took a deep breath. "Is he involved in this?"

"His name has come up here lately and I'm hearing rumors that his mom might have been more involved with Jacob than just a housekeeper. I need to flush that out a bit. Quentin lives there with his mom and I don't want to be outnumbered."

Tabor laughed. "I don't blame you. Quentin can be mouthy. Maybe he'll behave better with his mom there."

"Somehow, I don't think so." Conrad leaned back in his chair and stretched. "What did you think of the hairs you found in the vehicle?"

"A couple were really long, and I'd say they're blonde, but it could be a light brown or gray. It's hard to tell with just one hair. Asher was right, though. There was a lot of blood in the rear cargo area. I don't need a lab to tell me that."

"Sounds like we have a female accomplice. I don't think a woman could have moved Jacob alone."

"Quentin and his mom?" Tabor raised his eyebrows.

Conrad shrugged.

"Holler when you're ready to go," Tabor said as he walked back toward his desk just as Conrad's cell phone rang.

"Hey, Ned. I got your email. Thanks for that. I appreciate it."

"Sure," Ned Carey said. "I just wanted to give you a heads up that Jeremiah is in town. I guess when I stopped taking his calls, he decided he could make a trip to Spicetown."

"Well, I think it's for the best. The coroner's office is going to need someone to make arrangements for Jacob and it's a whole lot easier to do it from here."

"You won't feel that way when you see him," Ned said. "He's pretty fired up and I don't think he'll be useful to anyone in his state of mind."

"What's he upset about? You said this morning that he doesn't know about the will."

"He doesn't know any specifics, but he knows he's not in charge, so I think he's jumping to the conclusion that he's cut out completely."

"Well, that's not true. Won't he get the proceeds of the business and the new house? I haven't finished reading all of it, but if he's the only living family, he would get whatever cash is left after the bills are paid. Right?"

"Not in this case. He gets the house out on Lavender Lane and that's it. The problem with that, is that house isn't paid for."

"Oh," Conrad moaned. "Jeremiah just inherited a debt."

"Exactly. He doesn't realize that yet, but that's why I'm calling. He's in an ill humor now. It's only going to get worse."

Conrad rubbed his hand over his face. "Great."

"I'm concerned that he's going to try to give Annie Radford a hard time. I didn't tell him Annie is inheriting anything, but he seems to suspect that on his own. He asked directly if she was named. If he goes out to her trailer raising cane, her son, Quentin, is going to twist him into a pretzel."

"I'm headed out by there this morning anyway. I'll talk to Annie and give her a heads-up not to answer the door to him. She can just call me, and I'll pick him up."

"I don't know if he has a key to the house on Parsley Street, but he may be headed there, too."

"We've processed the house, but I'd prefer he not disturb things, especially since he's not inheriting it in the end. Does he even know about the new house? I didn't think he and Jacob were talking."

"I don't know," Ned said. "Probably not unless he keeps in touch with someone here in town."

"Well, thanks for calling, Ned. I'll keep an eye out."

"Okay, Connie. See you tomorrow."

Conrad pocketed his cell phone and strolled down the hallway toward the dispatch cubicle.

"Georgie?" Conrad leaned across the counter that separated the lobby from the officer's desks. "Do you know Jeremiah Hart? Jacob Hart's son?"

"I know about him, but I'm not sure I would recognize him now. I haven't seen him since he was little." Officer Georgia Marks leaned forward and patted Briscoe's head.

"Well, he's supposed to be in town, so if he should happen to stop in, please let me know. I'd like to talk to him."

"Sure thing, Chief." Georgia looked down at Briscoe who had his head cocked to one side. "I think your partner is ready for some action."

Conrad chuckled. "I can't take him with me this morning.   He'll have to rely on you for entertainment."

"I can't dance," Georgia said to Briscoe as she placed her palm under his jaw to tip his face up to meet her gaze. "And I'm not much of a singer either."

"Hang in there, Briscoe. I hope I won't be gone too long." Conrad tapped his palms on the counter and spun around at the sound of his name.

"Hey, Gerald." Conrad reached out his hand to shake hands with Gerald Landry.

"Can I talk to you a minute?"

"Sure. Come on back to my office. I've got a few minutes. I was just getting ready to leave, but Officer Tabor is finishing up yet. What can I do for you?" Conrad fell back in his desk chair as Gerald sat timidly in the visitor's chair across from Conrad's desk.

"You asked me to bring my gun into the office."

"Yes," Conrad nodded, wondering where Gerald was carrying the gun.

"I don't have it."

"You don't have it?" Conrad's eyebrows went up in question and he waited for an explanation.

"No. It's not in the case and I asked Miriam about it. She said Jacob borrowed it over a month ago and she'd forgotten to tell me."

"Is that something that's happened before? I mean, has Jacob ever asked to borrow your gun before?"

"Never. As far as I know he has never owned a gun and never wanted one. I asked Miriam if he said why he needed it and she said Jacob didn't give her any explanation. He dropped by the house one day when I was at the doctor and told her that was why he had stopped by. She just thought I'd consented already, and it was arranged. Later, when I got home, she forgot all about it."

"How odd," Conrad said with a wrinkled forehead and a scrunched nose. "I don't suppose you have the serial number with you?"

"It's at home on the certificate. I can get it for you."

"Yes, that will help." Conrad stood up to communicate that the interview had ended.

"I would guess it's somewhere in Jacob's house." Gerald shrugged.

"I didn't see it, but I'll look again. I've heard that Jeremiah is in town today, so he might be over at the house, too."

Gerald's eyes widened in alarm. "I sure hope he doesn't find it. I don't think that young man is mentally stable."

"Really? Why do you say that?" Conrad scratched his head but remained standing.

"Just from things Jacob has told me over the years. I haven't seen the boy."

"Well, you may see him soon. Thanks for coming by Gerald and you give me a call when you get the serial number."

Gerald rose slowly from his chair but before he could straighten, he lowered himself back down. "Conrad. I think I may know why Jacob wanted that gun."

"And why is that, Gerald?"

"Jacob told me that Tim Grace was involved with some shady characters. There were guys coming into the office to see him and Jacob thought something other than tax work was going on. I think he was a little frightened. He might have taken the gun up to the office."

"How long ago did he mention this to you?"

"When he started building the house," Gerald said. "We've been talking a lot more often since he started on that project. That last night, the night we were out at the house, he said he was thinking about retiring and just closing the office down."

"Had he discussed that with Tim? That would put Tim out of business, too. He'd have to open his own place or go to work for someone else."

"Yeah, but I don't think Jacob would talk to him about it. I don't think the two of them talked at all anymore."

"So, these shady characters," Conrad said, sitting back down in his office chair. "Any idea what made them shady? Did they look like criminals or say something that made Jacob suspicious?"

"I'm not sure," Gerald said frowning. "I got the impression that maybe Jacob overheard some conversation and knew they weren't talking about financial planning or taxes. He didn't indicate it was their appearance, but they were men that he didn't know, so probably not locals." Gerald rose from his seat fully and straightened the front of his jacket. "I'll call the serial number in and let me know if you find it. I hope it hasn't been stolen."

"I will, Gerald. Thanks."

Gerald waved over his shoulder as he walked out of Conrad's office door.

§

"Can we please just go?" Tonya Grace leaned forward across Jacob Hart's desk and stretched forward. "You can just close the office. There's nobody here and we can just run out there really quick."

"Just go. You don't need me. I've got too much to do today. I've got people coming later and I'm not finished with their file." Tim Grace didn't look up from his laptop screen but gave her a dismissive wave.

"I don't want to go by myself."

The exaggerated whine in her tone made Tim expel a heavy sigh before looking up from his work. "Not now, Tonya."

"Just great," Tonya muttered in disgust. "Here comes the mayor. You're not going to get anything done now. See, we should have gotten out of here when we could."

"I don't know what she wants. I've already offered to help with her taxes, but she doesn't want my help."

"Maybe she's changed her mind!" Tonya hopped up from Jacob's chair and walked around his desk to greet Cora as she walked through the door. "Hi, Mayor!"

"Hello, you two. How are things?" Cora Mae fluffed her windblown hair.

"Just great. How are you doing?" Tonya motioned for Cora to take a seat.

"Well, I know you are very busy, but I just stopped in to ask a favor if I could. I won't take much of your time."

"Sure, Mayor." Tim stood up from his desk and walked around to the front of the desk and leaned his hip on the corner. "What can we do for you?"

Cora looked up at Tim and shrugged slightly. "Well, I know there's a file up here on my past business with Jacob and I was hoping you would give that to me. I've been thinking about it and it's worrying me a little. I'd like to have it for safekeeping and it also might have information in it that will help me with future tax returns. Do you think you could pull that file for me?"

"Ah, Mayor, I don't know," Tim said, pushing his palms into the small of his back. "We don't really keep files anymore."

Cora raised her eyebrows. "No?"

"Nah, everything is electronic nowadays. Printing it all out would take a while to do. Do you need it right away?"

"Oh, you don't need to print everything out for me," Cora said, waving her hands. Reaching in her purse, she pulled out the thumb drive that Amanda had given her when she told her about her plans to pick up her files. "Can you just copy it to my drive?"

Tim's gaze traveled over Cora's head as he seemed to search the blank wall behind her for a response. "Uh, well, I guess."

"I can do that for you," Tonya said, reaching over to snatch the drive from Cora's hand. "It should just take a few minutes." Tonya walked around Jacob's desk and sat down.

"Thank you," Cora smiled. "I didn't want to bother anyone, but time is getting short."

Tim nodded and then walked back around his desk to answer his ringing phone. "Hart and Grace Tax Service. How can I help you?"

"Found it! Do you want everything, Mayor?" Tonya asked Cora. "It goes way back."

"Yes, please. After you copy it, I'd like it deleted, if you would. I'm not comfortable with my personal information remaining on the computers."

Tim turned away from the ladies and lowered his voice. "Sure. I can come by after work, but I'm working late tonight. It might be eight o'clock. Will you still be at the station then?"

"I'll have to ask Tim about that," Tonya whispered to Cora.

"Okay. Sure. See you then." Tim hung up his desk phone and turned to face Cora.

"Honey, can I delete the mayor's file after I copy it?" Tonya pointed to Cora. "I didn't know if that was okay."

"No," Tim said, shaking his head. "We have to keep everything for ten years in case something comes up because your returns would show that the business completed them."

Cora nodded with a furrowed brow. Her ultimate goal had failed. "Thank you, dear." Cora reached across the desk to take the small drive from Tonya's outstretched hand. "I'll be on my way now. Don't work too hard."

Sheri Richey

CHAPTER 21

"Miss Annie." Conrad tipped his head in greeting when Annie Radford answered her trailer door.

"Hello, Chief. How can I help you? Do you want to come in?" Annie backed up into her living room and pushed the front door open. "Come on in."

"Thank you," Conrad said as he stepped into Annie's living room with Eugene Tabor on his heels. "This is Officer Tabor. We hate to bother you, but we just had a few questions. Is your son at home?"

"Quentin? No, he's not here. Did you need to talk to him?"

"Well, I can catch up with him later. I do have a few things I needed to ask you about." Conrad walked toward the kitchen when Annie reached up and opened a top cabinet.

"Can I get you two some coffee? I've got some made."

"No, thank you, ma'am." Tabor said softly.

"No, thank you. I've got some out in the car," Conrad said as he shook his head. "We won't be but a minute."

"Well, have a seat. How can I help?" Annie sat down at the kitchen table as Conrad pulled out a chair to sit. Officer Tabor remained standing near the front door.

"I needed to ask you a little about the past, Annie. Folks are telling me that Jeremiah got bent out of shape over something between you and Jacob. Do you know anything about that?"

"Oh, Chief, that was ages ago. Jeremiah and Jacob always had trouble between them, but back before Margie died, Jeremiah found something in storage. It was something that Jacob wrote to someone named Annie or maybe someone wrote to Jacob. I don't remember exactly, but it wasn't even me. It was someone he knew back in college. Margie told me about it because she was afraid Jeremiah would say something to me. He was just a teenager then, but I did see him when I visited with Margie sometimes."

"Did she show it to you?" Conrad pulled his pen from his front pocket to make a note.

"No. She just warned me in case Jeremiah tried to accuse me of something. She said it was written before she even met Jacob and it was nothing. She laughed about it, but she was distressed that they were fighting. Jacob would just shut down and not talk to Jeremiah when he went off on a tangent. Margie wanted them to sit down calmly and discuss it, but Jacob refused. Maybe Jeremiah read that as guilt, but it's really just Jacob's personality. He doesn't like confrontation."

"Did Jeremiah ever say anything to you?" Conrad said.

"No, never did. It reared it's ugly head again after Margie died though. From what I hear, Jeremiah made some comments to some people here in town about it right after Margie's funeral. I hear tell he made some snide remarks that Jacob and I could be together now and even said things about Quentin. He still had it in his head that his father and I had been a couple, many years ago. Maybe he still thinks that." Annie shrugged her shoulders and shook her head.

"But you never have been?"

"No!" Annie chuckled. "I didn't even meet Jacob until Sam and I started attending his church. I knew about his business downtown, but I'd never met the man. Margie was in my Sunday School class and we became friends. Jeremiah was just a young boy, so he thinks I've been around forever, I guess." Annie laughed.

"What about your relationship recently?" Conrad glanced at Annie over his reading glasses. "Were you two friends?"

"I wouldn't say that. I worked for Jacob. We had a working relationship. About a month after Margie died, I saw Jacob at church and asked him how he was doing. He said he was having a hard time and needed some help around the house. He asked me if I knew anyone I could recommend."

"That's when you started cleaning for him?"

"Yes. Doc Mason was closing the office in May that year and I was thinking that I would probably need some part-time work to get by, so I volunteered. I told Jacob I would do it and we worked out a deal."

"Did Quentin know Jacob and Jeremiah?" Conrad leaned back in his chair and glanced over his shoulder at Tabor.

"Quentin and Jeremiah went to school together, but Quentin was older, so they really didn't have any relationship at all. They knew each other. It was much the same with Jacob. Quentin saw him at church when he was a boy and knew that I was friends with Margie, but that's all."

"So, Quentin didn't ever see or talk to Jacob since he's been back home with you."

"Since he got released from jail?" Annie raised her eyebrows. "Not that I know about, but I guess he's a grown man. He could have talked to Jacob, but he didn't tell me about it."

"I'll check with him. Just to be clear, Annie, you and Jacob have never had a personal relationship of any kind. Is that correct?"

Annie tossed her head back and laughed. "That's correct, Chief. Absolutely not. Now wouldn't we have made an odd pair?"

"I don't know," Conrad said as he slipped his reading glasses back in his shirt pocket. "What makes you say that?"

"Jacob's all educated and professional with his fancy house and business. I'm just a simple girl living in the sticks."

"Speaking of houses, did Jacob talk to you about the new house he was building and what plans he had for the house on Parsley Street?"

"He told me he wanted to deed it to me." Annie clasped her hands in front of her on the table and leaned forward. "I told him I didn't want it. I'm just fine with what I have right here, and I don't take charity."

"I'm sure he meant it as a gift, maybe from Margie." Conrad shrugged.

"No matter," Annie said, shaking her head as she looked down at her hands. "I told him I wouldn't take it."

"Okay, Annie. I appreciate your time. Do you know when I might catch Quentin?"

"He's at work right now. You might catch him there if he doesn't have any deliveries, but I'll give you his number, so you can call him." Annie tore off a piece of paper from a notepad by her phone. "He works down at Freddie's Auto Parts store south of town."

Conrad nodded and thanked Annie as he led Tabor back to his car.

"Chief, you want to run out to Freddie's now?"

"Yeah, we'll take a drive that way and check it out," Conrad said as he slid into the driver's seat and waited for Eugene to shut the passenger door. "I've got a report that Quentin went to see Jacob at his office after he was released from jail."

"Ms. Radford must not know about it," Tabor said as he clicked his seatbelt.

"Maybe not."

"What did you think about Ms. Radford and Jacob? Think she's telling the truth about them not having a thing?" Tabor leaned forward in his seat and looked at Conrad.

Conrad chuckled. "It's hard to believe a man that is careful with his money would just give a house away. That seems out of character for Jacob unless there's something I don't know. What did you think? Did you believe her?"

"It sounds crazy to me, too. She seemed convincing on her side of it, but I think maybe the feeling wasn't mutual."

"Oh, you think maybe Jacob wanted something more from Annie?" Conrad tilted his head and gave it some thought. "Like unrequited love? Jacob wanted Annie to have the house because she wouldn't have him?"

Tabor shrugged. "Jacob could have always had a crush on her, but she was his wife's best friend, you know. After the wife died, he gave it a try to she shot him down. He could have talked her into cleaning house for him so he could keep her around, pretend she was taking care of him."

Conrad smiled and nodded his head. "Anything is possible. We can only get one side of that story."

"Unless Quentin knows something." Tabor held up his index finger. "She may not want us talking to him because he could put another spin on things."

"I noticed she seemed reluctant at first when we asked if Quentin was home. I thought it was because she was afraid, we wanted to question him about something he'd done. At the end she seemed okay with us contacting him."

"Yeah, but I bet she gives him a call as a heads-up." Tabor held onto the dash of the car when Conrad hit the large potholes pulling into the gravel parking lot at Freddie's Auto Parts.

"It looks pretty quiet here today," Conrad said as he parked at the front door. "Let's see if we can find out."

§

"I do appreciate the advice," Cora Mae said to Amanda as she slipped on her jacket. "You were right about everything being electronic. That was the first thing they did. They said it would take too long to copy all of my file because there were so many years. It's really scary to use these services. All of my personal information is sitting right up there in that little building and I can't do anything about it. I always trusted Jacob with it, but now I feel very vulnerable."

233

"At least you have copies of everything in case you need it for something. Why did Tim Grace say he couldn't delete your files? Even if something comes up on them later, he can't represent you with the IRS." Amanda turned to her computer and pulled up a search page. "And ten years, that doesn't make any sense. They don't go back ten years on individual taxes. It's only seven years."

"How do you know all this?"

"I was reading all about record keeping when I helped Bryan with his taxes. There's nothing about retaining returns for ten years. He made that up."

Cora laughed. "Perhaps I should try again then. I could ask Ned Carey to write a letter to Tim Grace requesting he delete my information—"

"Or you'll report him for identify theft to the IRS!" Amanda pointed to her computer monitor. "It says right here on the IRS website that you can report tax preparers with this form."

Cora bristled and shook her head. "I don't have any evidence Tim stole anything. I don't think I want to go that far."

"But even if he told you he deleted your files; you'd never know if he did or not."

"Hmm, that's true. I guess I need to try to put it out of my mind. It's not something I can fix." Cora tossed the strap of her purse over her shoulder. "It all gave me a weird feeling. Tim took a phone call while I was there, and I think it was the Chief asking him to come down to the station. Even

Tonya acted odd. She's always been warm and friendly, but I got the feeling she was trying to get me out of there. I was very uncomfortable. I can't put my finger on it, but something was off."

"What are you going to do about your taxes?"

"I'm going home right now to do them myself!" Holding on to her purse strap, Cora gave a curt nod. "If I don't show up for work one day, you'll know the IRS came and carted me away!" After a flamboyant exit, Cora Mae's laughter trickled out when she pushed through the back door of City Hall.

Sheri Richey

CHAPTER 22

Pulling open the grimy glass entrance door, Conrad squinted as he looked around the store. There was no one behind the counter and no customers in the aisles. Conrad cupped his hands around his mouth and shouted, "Freddie! Freddie, are you in here?"

"Yep, yep, yep."

Conrad heard shuffling from behind the back wall of the counter.

"Yep! Oh! Hey, Chief. I'm here. Hey! How are you?" Freddie stepped up on a stool and reached over the checkout counter to extend his hand, then scowled as he glanced at his palm and pulled it back. "Sorry about that. How can I help the PO-lice today?" Freddie giggled and rocked back and forth.

"We're here looking for Quentin. Quentin Radford. Is he around?" Conrad glanced down the dark dirty aisles of auto parts behind the counter.

"Yep, yep. He's around back. Let me get him for you." Freddie hopped off of his stool and waddled behind the back wall calling for Quentin. "Radford!"

Freddie Gaines was an extremely short man with bright red hair and noticeably bowed legs that made him rock from one side to the other when he walked, however, his cheerful, bubbly personality was his most memorable characteristic.

"Oh," Quentin said as he wiped his hands off on a filthy oil-stained rag. "Hey, Chief. What's up?"

"Just need a minute of your time, Quentin. Is it okay if he steps outside with us?" Conrad held out his arm to guide Quentin to the door.

"Yep, sure Chief." Freddie waved his arm vigorously to shoo them towards the door. "Whatever you need."

"I didn't do nothin'," Quentin said with his hands raised in front of him. Glancing fearfully at Freddie, he straightened his shoulders. "And I don't know nothin'."

Conrad chuckled. "Relax, Quentin. I'm not accusing you of anything. I'm working on Jacob Hart's case and your name came up. That's all."

"My name!" Quentin tossed the oily rag on the counter.

"It's probably about that gun that Jack Rabbit found," Freddie said, waving his index finger in the air. "He thought it looked like yours." Leaning his elbows on the counter, Freddie looked at

Conrad. "Is that right, Chief? Jack Rabbit has already been by telling us about it. Quentin ain't got nothin' to do with that."

"Can we step outside, Quentin?" Conrad held his arm out toward the door again to guide Quentin forward.

Quentin nodded reluctantly and followed the Chief through the front door of the shop with Tabor close on his heels.

"What's this about, Chief?" Quentin stood in front of Conrad's squad car with his arms crossed over his chest.

"Just came from your mom's. I wanted to ask you about what happened between you and Jacob when you got out of jail. Can you tell me about it?"

"Not much to tell," Quentin said as he looked down and kicked at the gravel. "He tried to get all involved in my legal issues and I told him to mind his own business. That's about all there was to it."

"Why didn't you want his help?" Conrad leaned against his car and squinted up at Quentin. "He was trying to get you a good lawyer, wasn't he?"

"That's what he told Ma, but he was trying to set me up to go away to prison. The lawyer he tried to hook me up with was married to Clyde Schofield's aunt. You think he's going to help me beat a battery charge against his wife's nephew? He was a ringer. He was going in there trying to get me to take a plea and do ten years in state prison. I fired him as soon as I found out what was going on and I told Ma about it."

"Did she talk with Jacob about it?"

"I don't know. She didn't believe he did it intentionally. She said he couldn't have known about any of that family connection. She doesn't think he can do any wrong, but I think he was trying to get rid of me. When I got out, I went over to his office and told him to stay away from me. That's all there was to it, really. We never talked again."

Conrad shrugged. "Why would Jacob try to get you sent up? Was there bad blood between you?"

"He always had a thing for my mom. I think he thought if he got rid of me, she would need his help." Quentin looked down and pushed his toe into the gravel. "We were doing just fine. We didn't need him."

"Has he tried to help your mom before?" Conrad opened his car door and grabbed his sunglasses. The sun was directly over Quentin's head and shining right into his eyes.

"He'd always try to give her money. That's why she started working for him. She ain't gonna take a handout."

"Did they have a personal relationship of some sort at any time? Folks are telling me that Jacob's son thought they were seeing each other. Dating, you know. Was that ever the case?"

"I know Jeremiah tried to spread that rumor years ago. That ain't the case, though. Ask her. She'll tell ya."

"Okay," Conrad said as he crossed his arms over his chest. "Can you tell me where you were the evening of April first? It was a Wednesday."

Quentin shrugged. "I don't know, at home, I guess. I work until six o'clock and I go home."

"You don't know? Or you were at home?" Conrad leaned his hip against his car.

"I was home. I don't remember nothin' special about Wednesday. It was just like any other night." Quentin tossed his hands out to his sides and let the palms slap against his legs.

"Your mom there with you?" Conrad raised an eyebrow. He hadn't asked Annie her whereabouts that night.

"Yeah. She's always there makin' dinner when I get home."

"One more thing," Conrad said pushing away from his car to stand. "What about your gun? Freddie said Jack Rabbit Robbins thought the gun he found was yours?"

"Nah, Chief. That was the old days," Quentin said with a dismissive wave of his hands. "I sold it years ago. Jack Rabbit just thought about it because he knew I had a Sig Saar back in the day."

"Who did you sell it to?" Conrad glanced over at Officer Tabor and saw he was taking notes.

"Some gun dealer. There was a gun show over in Red River a few years back and I sold it to one of the dealers there."

"You had papers on it. It was a clean sale?" Conrad leaned his arms on top of his open car door.

"Yeah, it was my daddy's gun. I didn't want to sell it, but we needed the money. It's all legal and stuff."

"Okay. That's all for now, Quentin. I appreciate you giving us a minute."

Quentin nodded and stepped up on the sidewalk in front of the door. "You know, Chief. If you're looking for someone that hated Jacob Hart, you need to look close at Jeremiah. I don't know where he is now, but I know he has a powerful hate for his daddy."

Conrad nodded. "Thanks, Quentin."

Quentin yanked open the door to Freddie's Auto Parts as Tabor opened the passenger door of Conrad's car. "Quentin has sure settled himself since the last time I saw him."

"Yeah," Conrad said as he dropped down into the driver's seat. "I didn't expect a rational conversation. Maybe he's matured some since I saw him last."

"Or maybe he's just stopped drinking." Tabor pulled the door shut and smirked.

§

Cora Mae sat down at the desk in her spare bedroom and arranged all the information she had gathered for Jacob Hart to do her taxes. She had no idea what he did with her end of year credit card statements and mortgage forms, but he had always asked for them. Logging into her email account, she clicked the link to the program that Amanda had forwarded to her and began setting up an account online for herself.

Marmalade meowed and jumped up on the bed in the spare bedroom after inspecting all the corners of the room. Cora rarely opened the door to the guest room and Marmalade had to first inspect and confirm that nothing new had sneaked in under her watch.

It felt awkward to sit at Bing's old desk. George Bingham had used the small desk only on rare occasions, but it was where he had worked on their income taxes so many years ago. She should have asked him about them. She should have been involved. It had been too easy to let him take care of those financial matters, and now she was at a disadvantage. When her self-doubt began to take over, she brushed it off and took a deep, cleansing, confident breath. She could do this.

The online program was very informative and instead of seeing a grid with many boxes as she expected, it was a simple questionnaire that walked her through each area with easy questions seeking yes or no answers. Pausing to enter her information when prompted, she hovered over the question marks and read the explanation for each area of the return. Now she understood how

Amanda had learned so much in a single weekend helping Bryan.

Cora Mae looked over at Marmalade sprawled out on the guest bed and cocked her ear towards the door. She thought she heard something, but Marmalade didn't confirm it, so Cora continued her data entry. As she neared the end of the tax program, she began to wonder how much she had paid Jacob Hart over the last fifteen years when she should have been doing this herself. If she had met this challenge headfirst back then, she wouldn't be dealing with the uneasy feeling that the Hart & Grace Tax Service had possession of all her personal information.

Cora's head jerked again, and Marmalade raised up her head. Both of them looked toward the bedroom door. Pushing back her chair, Cora stood and continued to listen. "Is someone here?" Marmalade ignored the question but pushed herself up to a sitting position and then jumped off the bed. Cora followed Marmalade into the living room and glanced out the front window. A small dark sedan sat out front next to the curb in front of her house.

Not recognizing the car, Cora looked through the peephole in the door and saw someone walking up her driveway. With her hand on the deadbolt, Cora stopped as she realized it was Tonya Grace. Strangely, her first instinct was to flee.

Tiptoeing into the kitchen, she picked up her cell phone and stood in her foyer waiting for Tonya's knock. Bing had always encouraged her to listen to her instincts and although she couldn't explain the foreboding she felt at knowing Tonya was approaching her house, she had learned to take those feelings seriously.

With her index finger poised over the dial pad in her phone, Tonya rapped softly at her front door. Cora Mae froze and stared at her finger as she debated whether to call the police department. What would she say?

The rapping grew stronger as Tonya began to call out to her. In that moment of panic, Cora realized what her subconscious was trying to tell her and she hit the speed dial number for the PD. Leaving a quick message with Officer Sam Crawford at the dispatch desk, she knew someone would be there shortly, so she needed to keep Tonya talking.

"Tonya, dear?" Cora called through the locked door. "Is everything okay?"

"Mayor! Oh, I'm so glad you're home. I hate to bother you, but could I talk to you for just a minute? It's about your taxes."

"Certainly, dear. I haven't looked at them yet. Is there something wrong?"

"Could I come in for a minute? Please?"

The pleading in Tonya's voice was tugging at Cora's heart strings, but she still had her wits about her. Peeking through the peephole again, she looked to see if Tonya held anything in her hands. Seeing no gun or weapon, she flipped the deadbolt.

"Come in," Cora said holding the screen door open and ushering Tonya through the door. Leaving the front door ajar, she patted Tonya's back and led her to the kitchen. "Can I get you a cup of tea?"

CHAPTER 23

Conrad pulled out a chair that was tucked under the table in the interview room and invited Tim Grace to take a seat.

"I'm sorry it's so late, Chief. I'm just swamped right now, and I've been working late all week."

"I understand that. I know it's a really bad time for this to happen, but it really can't wait." Conrad pulled a pen from his shirt pocket.

"Happy to help, Chief." Tim clasped his hands on the table in front of him.

"Let me get a little background for starters." Conrad patted his pockets for his reading glasses. "I've talked to a lot of people already, but I'd like to get your take on how the business is set up. Can you tell me a little history on that?"

"Me and Jacob?"

Conrad nodded.

"Well, Jacob was looking to hire an assistant. This was back in '97, I think, and I was looking for a job. I applied and he invited me to interview. It was just an office clerk type of job. You know, make copies, and answer the phone. That type of stuff. We hit it off pretty well and he hired me. That's how it started."

"Okay," Conrad said, crossing his foot up over his opposite knee, creating a table for his notepad. "How did that evolve into the business name changing?"

Tim chuckled. "Jacob had a vision. He wanted me to register for classes and get my accounting degree. I liked the work, but he just couldn't accept the fact that I don't like going to school."

"Did you and Jacob do any formal paperwork?"

"No, we never did," Tim shrugged. "We talked about it, but he never followed through."

"When was the last time you actually talked to Jacob? I mean, other than to say hello or goodbye."

"Gosh, I don't know. Jacob wasn't real chatty. We talked a little about our houses that last week he worked. I told him about a sale on lighting fixtures over in Paxton that Tonya and I were going to check out. Nothing heavy."

"Did he ever mention his son, Jeremiah, to you?"

"Nah, not really. They aren't real close." Tim shrugged and looked around the room.

"Do you know anyone that was angry with Jacob? Any clients that he had disagreements with?"

"There are always a few that think they should get more money back," Tim said with a smirk. "Nothing that made me think we were in any danger. Do you think it was a customer that did this?"

"When was the last time you and Jacob had an argument?"

"We didn't!" Tim held his hands out. "We just each did our own thing."

Conrad took a deep breath. "Where were you last Wednesday evening?"

"Wednesday?" Tim looked at the ceiling. "I'd have to check with Tonya. I really don't remember. I probably worked late. Yeah, yeah, I did. I called Tonya and had her go out to the house and check on things during the day because I had to work late and wouldn't be able to go out there when I got off. I think that was Wednesday. I'm not sure."

"Do you—." Conrad looked at the interview room door when he heard a soft tap. "Excuse me a minute."

Tim Grace nodded as Conrad pushed back his chair and stepped outside the interview room door.

"Chief, I'm sorry to bother you," Officer Sam Crawford whispered. "I just thought you'd want to know that the Mayor called and she says that Jacob's murderer is on her front porch." Sam looked over his shoulder toward the lobby. "I sent

Hudson over there because he was closest, but Wink is backing him up."

Conrad scowled. "Who is on her porch?"

Sam's eyes went wide. "Tonya Grace. Mayor says to tell you it's the fingernail."

Conrad's eyebrows shot up. "Call Wink and tell him to bring Tonya in. If she argues, just have him tell her she's being detained for questioning. Knock on the door when they get here. I'm going back in with Tim."

"Gotcha, Chief."

§

"I was just going to make myself some tea," Cora said once Tonya was seated at her kitchen table.

"Oh, no. I'm fine. I just needed to talk to someone. I'm afraid for Tim. I'm afraid something bad is going to happen to him and I don't know who to talk to about it. He won't tell the police, but the Chief called today and asked him to come in. He's down there right now. Maybe the Chief already knows about the trouble he's in, but he's afraid to talk about it. I'm hoping you can help him."

"Oh, dear!" Cora Mae filled her tea kettle with water. "What trouble is he in? I don't understand. Is someone angry with him? Is he receiving threats?"

"He got into some business deal with some guys I don't know. He won't even explain it to me, but the business deal went badly. They're coming after him. I think it's all tied into Jacob. Tim won't tell me everything, but I'm sure he didn't mean for anyone to get hurt."

Marmalade meowed loudly in the middle of the kitchen and then headed down the hallway toward the front door. Tonya turned around in her chair.

"Oh, don't mind her," Cora said with a wave of her hand. "She's just saying hello to you."

Tonya relaxed when she saw Marmalade leave the room, but Cora knew Marmalade loved to play greeter and hoped it was Wink sneaking in the front door and not Tim Grace's enemies.

"Tim killed Jacob?" Cora turned around and leaned back against her kitchen counter. "Because Jacob was going to turn him in?"

"It was an accident. I know it was. Tim wouldn't ever hurt anybody. He's just scared. He's so jumpy. There's a lot of pressure on him right now."

Cora Mae saw the sleeve of a Spicetown police officer pressed against the wall of her hallway near the doorway to her kitchen. She wasn't sure who it was, but those details could wait. Walking over to the table, she pulled out a chair to sit by Tonya.

"Accidents happen. I hope he didn't mean Jacob any harm, but it doesn't mean he isn't responsible for his death. He needs to take responsibility for his actions, just as you do."

"That's why I'm here. I know Tim will want to do the right thing, but I want you to understand that he's not a murderer. It was all an accident.

Tim got a gun, but he doesn't know anything about guns. He was just scared. He said he shot Jacob, but he thought he was somebody else. You've got to believe him."

"Were you there when all this happened?"

"No, but he called me. He was so shaken. That's how I know it was a horrible mistake. It was wrong for us to cover it up, but we had to do something."

"Ms. Grace," Wink said as he stepped into Cora's kitchen doorway. "I need you to come down to the station and make a statement now."

Tonya looked startled and then accusingly at Cora Mae. "Did you call them?"

Before Cora could respond, Wink was at Tonya's elbow helping her out of her chair and Officer Darren Hudson framed the doorway. "Evening, Mayor."

"Good evening and thank you," Cora said quietly as Wink led Tonya to the front door.

"Anytime, Mayor. Be sure and lock up now," Officer Hudson said with a twinkle in his eye as he pulled Cora Mae's front door closed behind him.

§

As Conrad slipped back into the interview room, Sam hurried back to the dispatch cubicle. "Sorry about that."

"No worries."

"Now, where was I?" Conrad crossed his leg back over his ankle and looked directly at Tim. "Where was your wife, Tonya, on Wednesday night?"

"Home."

"How do you know that if you were working late?" Conrad cocked his head.

"We talk. We text, you know. We keep in touch. If she'd gone anywhere, I'm sure she'd tell me. She's home most evenings. She has dance lessons after school until almost seven o'clock at night."

"Every night?"

"No, but she can tell you. I can't keep it all straight, but that's part of the reason I've always worked late. It's different in the summer, but when school is in, she's busy in the evenings and I try to stay out of the way."

"Tell me about the building lots out at Lavender Lane." Conrad leaned back in his chair. "Did you buy yours first and then Jacob?"

"Yeah, we were looking at the lots on Cumin Court first, but then when we heard they were opening another subdivision up next door, we waited. The lots on Lavender are cheaper."

"So, after you bought your lot, then Jacob became interested?"

"He may have already been looking like we were. We didn't talk about it." Tim shrugged and his upper lip curled.

"You weren't happy he chose to build so close to you."

"No, not really. I mean, I saw the guy all day long. I didn't want him to be my neighbor, too." Tim's volume raised as his hands went up in the air. "Would you?"

Conrad ignored his question. "Tell me about your clients. They're different from Jacob's, right?"

"Yeah. Yeah, we kept everything separate. Like I said, he did his thing and I did mine." Tim held up his palms and clasped his hands again.

"Exactly what is your thing? Do you handle different types of things? I wouldn't think taxes would keep you busy year around. What other financial services do you offer?"

"Oh, there's retirement planning and internal audits." Tim straightened up in his chair and leaned forward to count off his achievements on his fingers. "I do consulting, cash flow management, fraud reviews, business plans, risk assessments..."

"You can do that without an accounting degree or CPA license?"

"Sure," Tim said rocking back in his chair. "Anybody can do those things if they know enough about them."

"And how did you learn about them? Did you know all this when you started working with Jacob?" Conrad looked over the top of his reading glasses and saw Tim's puffed out chest deflate slightly.

"No, but I pay attention, you know." Tim leaned forward and nodded with feigned confidence. "I don't need to sit in a classroom. I learn from life around me, you know."

Conrad heard a twinge of defensiveness in Tim's proclamation and it was time to exploit that.

"And you learned a lot from Jacob? I bet in the beginning, back when he thought you were going to complete your education, he took some time to talk you through what he was doing. Didn't he show you how it was done? Didn't he try to take you under his wing and put your name on the door because he thought you were going to become his partner some day?

"He had high hopes for you. Was it all a scam? Did you know all along that you weren't going back to school? You were just planning to string old Jacob along and take his business without earning it?"

"Take his business? No way." Tim snarled and hunched his shoulders. "I don't need his old stuffy customers. I've cultivated my own. I make my own living without doing things his way. He didn't own me. He was always trying to tell me what to do or tell me I couldn't do something. I told him to mind his own business."

"And when he started butting into your business, did he threaten to turn you in? Report you to the feds?" Conrad leaned forward and raised his voice to match Tim's, hoping to goad him on. "Did he tell you that he wasn't going to let you work there anymore if you did that kind of work? Did he tell you he wanted to close the business down?"

Tim took a deep breath and sat back in his chair. "We had some words from time to time. We didn't always see eye to eye."

Conrad stood up when he heard a tap at the door. Slapping the notepad down on the table in front of Tim Grace, he tossed his pen on top of the notepad. "I'm going to give you some time to think about things and then I recommend you write up a statement as to what happened last Wednesday night. While you do that, I'm going to go talk to your wife."

Tim's gaze shot up in alarm. "Tonya's here?"

"I believe she's next door and I think she'll want to tell me the truth. Don't you?" Conrad turned to walk towards the interview room door.

"Wait, Chief. Can I talk to her?"

Conrad tossed back his head and laughed as he pulled the door shut behind him.

§

"Connie! I'm glad you called." Cora sat down at her kitchen table. "Sam probably thinks I'm crazy, but I just realized that when I saw Tonya at Tim's office earlier today, I saw she had fake fingernails on, and they were painted hot pink."

"Sam told me about the fingernail, and I figured that was what you meant."

"The nail on her right index finger is missing. It's not painted, and you can see glue or some kind of white residue on it. I noticed it when she handed me my thumb drive at Tim's office today, but it didn't register until she showed up at my door."

"You didn't open the door, right?"

"Well, yes, but I called Sam first. I knew someone was on the way. I couldn't let her get away. She kept saying it was about my tax files and she needed to talk to me."

"She could have had a weapon. You realize that you shouldn't have opened that door, right?" Conrad's teeth were gritted.

"That's neither here nor there. You can scold me later. It all turned out all right. She told me Tim killed Jacob!"

Conrad rolled his eyes and huffed. "Why did you go up to Tim's office today?"

"I wanted a copy of my old files. I thought I might need them to file my taxes this year. I wasn't Tim's client and I didn't want him having my personal information, especially not with all these rumors that he's not to be trusted."

"I understand," Conrad said.

"They were both acting uncomfortable today when I was there. It was awkward and I felt uneasy about it. When she started banging on my door, it finally all came together."

"Okay. Let me talk to Wink and then we'll see what she has to say. I've got Tim up here now, too."

"I can't believe they killed Jacob."

"Well, now, don't jump the gun," Conrad said. "We don't know that yet."

"I feel it in my bones," Cora said with a smile in her voice. "Does that count?"

Conrad laughed. "I'll put it in the pro column."

Hanging up the phone, Conrad saw Wink hovering outside his office. "Come on in, Wink. Tell me what happened out there."

CHAPTER 24

Late Friday morning, Cora Mae left the office a little early so she could run a few errands before meeting Conrad for lunch. After visiting the Sweet & Sour Spice Shop for Conrad's coffee, she rounded the corner and saw the planters lining the street were full of tiny spring buds while the rhododendrons in Paprika Park were bursting in bloom along the street's edge. Dog walkers and moms with strollers were walking on the circular path through the park as Cora crossed Paprika Parkway. Glancing down Fennel Street, Cora saw the silhouette of a large white bunny walking down the sidewalk in the block in front of her waving flyers over his head.

Cora Mae waved at the giant bunny when he turned around and started to walk towards her. "Saucy? Is that you in there?" Cora peered in the eye holes of the costume and squinted.

"Hey, Mayor. No, it's me. Jason. Jason Marks."

"Oh, Jason! How are you?" Cora squeezed his furry arm. "Are you passing out Easter flyers for Dot?"

"Yes, ma'am. We're having Easter dinner at the Caraway Café on Sunday. You should come! I think Mr. Salzman is going to help greet everyone at the door in the rabbit suit. He was busy today, so I'm working the sidewalk until Dorothy needs me inside."

"That's wonderful. I'm so glad Dot decided to do this, and you look fabulous as an Easter bunny, Jason." Cora Mae giggled when Jason nodded his large head.

"Yeah. Won't mom be proud?" Jason chuckled and then waved his large white paw at a passing car on Fennel Street.

"Well, don't let me keep you," Cora said. "I'm headed to the café myself. I'll let Dot know that you're doing a great job."

As Jason continued his stroll down Fennel Street, Cora pulled open the door to the Caraway Café and waved at Dorothy's husband, Frank, who was looking out the order window from the kitchen. Pulling out the chair to her favorite table in the front window, Dorothy Parish slid into the seat across from her. "Hey, Cora. Did you see Jason out there?"

"I did! I thought it was Saucy at first. It's such a cute idea. Really, Dot, you're brilliant." Cora smiled as Dorothy blushed.

"Thank you, but we'll have to wait and see what Sunday brings. I'm hoping Saucy can come work the door, but he's got a bit of a spring cold right now and feeling under the weather. I think having all those kids climbing all over him at the library got him sick."

"Oh, no," Cora said and quickly pulled out her notepad. She would need to check on Saucy and seeing Jason on the street had given her another thought she needed to jot down for later.

"Yeah, he said he's feeling better today though. He just wasn't up to working the sidewalk. With another day or so of rest, I hope he's able to come Sunday."

Cora nodded her head and pointed out the front window at Conrad chatting with the bunny. "That would make a good picture."

Dorothy laughed. "Spicetown Police Chief gives giant bunny a ticket for jay-hopping. I can see it on the front page of the Spicetown Star now!"

Cora Mae giggled as Conrad entered the restaurant.

"Uh oh," Conrad said as he removed his hat. "You ladies must be up to something."

Dorothy stood up and smiled. "I'll get you some tea, Cora. Coffee for you, Chief?"

"Nah, just water. Thanks." Conrad took the seat Dorothy had vacated and sat his hat in the seat beside him. "A busy week. I'm glad it's almost over."

"You look exhausted. Are all the loose ends tied up now?" Cora thanked a waitress who sat a pot of hot water on the table.

"All tied up with a bow on top. The Department of Justice is sending someone down this afternoon to talk to Tim, but otherwise, we're done. Tonya's already been transported to county jail and Tim will get moved later today."

"What does the Department of Justice want with Tim?"

"They've got a tax division that prosecutes tax fraud. They've got a big file on Tim already. Tabor's been in touch with them and when they found out we were holding him on murder charges, they wanted to join in."

"Did Tim and Tonya ever get their stories to match?" Cora Mae chuckled. "The last time we talked, they were each singing different tunes."

"Not really. I think Tonya is telling the truth as she knows it. She just wasn't in on it until after Jacob was dead. Tim had a lucrative operation going cheating the IRS and Jacob was going to shut it all down on him."

"I'm relieved to hear that she was seeking me out for real help with Tim's dilemma and not trying to kill me when she came to my house."

"Yeah, we got the security tapes from the Wasabi and it shows Tim getting out of Jacob's SUV. Tonya drove up right behind him in her car and Tim jumped in. She admits to helping him put

Jacob's body in the SUV and then dumping him in the park."

"That's when she lost the fingernail."

Conrad nodded. "Tim has changed his story from shooting at an animal in the bushes, to shooting at a bad guy that was after him, and now he says the whole thing was an accident. The gun just went off... twice!" Conrad tossed his head back and laughed. "He's quite the performer."

"I hear that Jeremiah did come to town and he is making arrangements for his father's burial. They are planning a service for next week."

"Yeah," Conrad said pointing at Cora's notepad. "What are you working on now? Pros and cons of an Easter parade for next year?"

"No, I just made a note to remind myself to call Saucy. Dot says he's been sick this week. I wanted to make sure and check on him in the morning."

"He may still be in shock over finding Jacob. He was pretty shaken about it," Conrad said.

"Yes, it rattled Rodney a bit too. I also made a note about *Harvey*, the movie. Have you seen it?"

"There's a movie called *Harvey*? I don't guess I have," Conrad frowned.

"It's an old movie. Jimmy Stewart has an imaginary friend who is a pooka, a giant rabbit. I saw Jason on the sidewalk when I was walking here, and I had this idea that *Harvey* might be a good play for the community center. We could use that rabbit suit again and it's a funny movie."

263

"What can I get you today?" Dorothy rested her hand on her hip. "The special is Lemon Pepper Rainbow Trout."

"That's for me," Conrad said giving Dorothy an index finger salute.

"Yes, that does sound good," Cora said.

"Coming up!" Dorothy tapped Conrad's empty coffee cup. "Have you quit the coffee?"

Conrad huffed. "Yeah, I'm trying to stay off it. Doctor's orders."

"We've got decaf if you want it. Just let me know," Dot said before she trotted off to the kitchen.

"That reminds me," Conrad said, pointing a finger at Cora. "I need to know about this coffee you've been giving me. What is it? I need to get some more."

"You like it?"

"Yeah. I go back to the doctor next Tuesday, but so far giving up the coffee has helped, so I'm going to stick with it."

Cora Mae reached in her large handbag and pulled out her earlier purchase. "You can get this at the Sweet & Sour Spice Shop. Karen always keeps it in stock." Cora placed the small bag of ground chicory in front of Conrad. "Now don't freak out. It's not actually coffee. I mean, it doesn't have any real coffee in it."

Conrad turned the package around and read the back. "Good grief! It's got *roots* in it and dandelions! What in the world--?"

"Now, Connie. Chicory is an herb. It's an herbal beverage, much like some of my teas. That's all."

"Your tea doesn't have roots and weeds in it!"

"It's plant-based, just like coffee!" Cora threw her hands up in frustration. "Chicory is actually good for digestion. It lowers blood sugar, lowers cholesterol and adds healthy fiber to your diet." Cora Mae stabbed her finger in the air at Conrad's face. If she could have reached him, she would have given him a hard poke in the chest.

"I would go eat some grass if I wanted healthy fiber." Conrad huffed and dropped the bag of chicory on the table between them. "I can't believe you've been giving me weeds to drink all this time and tricking me into thinking it's some kind of decaf coffee."

"Oh, hush. I knew you'd react like this. That's why I didn't tell you what it was. Can't you just accept the fact that it's healthy. It's all organic and it has made you feel better."

Conrad huffed and shook his head. "I liked it better when I didn't know what it was."

Cora pulled the napkin out from her silverware and placed it over her lap when she saw a waitress approaching with their lunches. "Don't sulk. When you get back to the office and put it in your cannister, you can pretend we never had this conversation."

"Good advice," Conrad said with a curt nod as he moved the chicory to the side of the table. "Consider it forgotten."

Cora Mae rolled her eyes and leaned back so the waitress could put down their lunch plates as Conrad thanked her.

"Now, back to that Easter parade idea you had," Cora said as she picked up her fork and pointed it at Conrad. "Do you think we should have an Easter parade next year?"

"Idea *I* had?" Conrad barked. "No. No, that wasn't me!" Conrad propped his elbow on the table to rest his forehead in his hand and groan as Cora Mae laughed.

"You know I love a parade!"

∞

★ The Spicetown Star ★

First Spicetown Merchant's Association Meeting Planned

-- Frank and Dorothy Parish, owners of the Caraway Café on Fennel Street, are hosting an informational meeting for Spicetown merchants interested in forming an association to offer benefits and support to each other.

Items of interest are business payroll services, tax preparation, group discounts for employee benefits such as health insurance, training classes and vendor opportunities, as well as group advertising rate savings.

All owners of Spicetown retail businesses and local service providers are invited.

Wed., May 1st, 7:00pm ~ Caraway Café

Sheri Richey

~ Author Note ~

When I began this novel, I thought only of the spring flowers and Easter eggs that would offset the imminent annual income tax deadline in the United States. What I find delightful about cozy mysteries, is the depiction of life as we *wish* it were, rather than how it is. A small town where everyone supports each other and a world where justice always prevails is a safe place to be.

As I complete this novel, many changes have transpired around the world to combat a deadly virus. The tax deadline has been postponed and public gatherings are canceled as our health and safety must be our primary concern. I hope your reading time is spent remembering simpler times when Easter eggs were hidden among the spring blooms and children were overjoyed at the sight of the Easter bunny.

Despite all these recent changes, I hope you all are safe and that you take the time to enjoy the spring flowers. At least they have bloomed as expected.

Sheri Richey

Cheesy Potato Skins

6 baked potatoes
1 cup cheddar cheese
Bacon pieces, cooked and crumbled
¼ cup melted butter
Salt

- Once the baked potatoes are cool enough, cut them in half and scoop out some of the center, leaving about a 1/2-inch layer of potato. (If you bake the potatoes in aluminum foil be sure to unwrap them right out of the oven so the skins don't get soggy.)
- Brush the potatoes with melted butter, sprinkle the skin side with salt, and put under the broiler for about 7 minutes or until they look a little browned.
- Add the cheese and bacon to the scooped side of the potatoes and broil again for 2 minutes or until the cheese is melted.
- Serve hot with a side of sour cream and/or sprinkle with chives.

Sheri Richey

If you think you may have been the victim of tax fraud by a tax preparer, please go to the IRS.gov website and search for Form 14157-A.

Choose tax help carefully!

For information to help you choose a tax preparer, the differences in credentials and qualifications, as well as how to submit a complaint regarding an unscrupulous tax return preparer, please go to and look at this site: www.irs.gov/chooseataxpro

I'd love to hear from you!

Find me on Facebook, Goodreads, Twitter, my website or join my email list for upcoming news!

www.SheriRichey.com

Sheri Richey